THE IRON JEHU

Also by Ray Hogan

TRAIL TO TUCSON
THE HOODED GUN
BLOODROCK VALLEY WAR
RECKONING IN FIRE VALLEY
MAN WHO KILLED THE MARSHAL
JACKMAN'S WOLF
CONGER'S WOMAN
MAN WITHOUT A GUN
HONEYMAKER'S SON
THE DOOMSDAY MARSHAL
THE YESTERDAY RIDER

THE IRON JEHU

RAY HOGAN

DOUBLEDAY & COMPANY, INC.
GARDEN CITY, NEW YORK
1976

All the characters in this book are fictitious,
and any resemblance to actual persons, living or
dead, is purely coincidental.

Library of Congress Cataloging in Publication Data

Hogan, Ray, 1908–
The iron jehu.

I. Title
PZ4.H716Ir [PS3558.03473] 813'.5'4

ISBN: 0-385-12409-0

Library of Congress Catalog Card Number: 76-10518

Printed in the United States of America

First Edition

for

LOIS

. . . my wife—and my life

THE IRON JEHU

1

"One thing for certain," Shanahan said, looking up from his battered, old roll-top desk, "you're sure going to have to watch your cussing if you aim to be around regular folks—specially younguns."

Sam Remington, standing in the doorway of the stage depot, open that young spring morning to admit the warm, fresh air, nodded slowly.

"Yeh, I been working on that. Man living around horses and mules most all his life sure can pile up some bad habits."

Tom Shanahan, squat, square-faced, who was station agent for the Valley Stage Lines at its Apache Springs office, sighed deeply. "Won't hardly be the same if you ain't around," he said hesitantly, stiff and awkward in his show of affection. "A man can get used to somebody in ten years."

Remington stirred, his gaze on the stagecoach being readied for the run south to Springerville. He'd be on it, making the ride for a last time—but as a passenger and not as the driver.

"It been that long?"

"Sure has. You showed up here for work on the first day of May '68."

"Ten years, almost to the day," Remington murmured. "It just don't seem that long."

Shanahan grunted his agreement, and shrugged. "Been a good ten years, Sam. Jeremiah Crenshaw and this here outfit of his owes you aplenty. Far as I'm concerned, you're the best goddammed jehu that ever drove a team of horses."

Remington shifted uncomfortably. "Obliged, Tom," he mumbled.

He was not a tall man, inclining to a stocky, thick-shouldered, muscular arm structure. His hair was iron gray, hung low on his neck, and the skin of his face, scoured by winds, hammered by sleet and rain, burned by the sun, had a brown, leathery texture while from the collar down, untouched by the elements, it was a startling white. His eyes were small, dark, and set to a constant squint. His hands, tough as a saddle skirt, were square shaped with strong, stubby fingers.

He was dressed for the trip to Springerville, and thence to Santa Fe where he planned to live with his daughter and her family, much the same as when he drove; brown cord pants, knee-high stovepipe boots with flat heels, checked flannel shirt closed at the collar with a string tie, black leather vest embellished with silver conchas. His one concession to the change in his life was a new hat—a pearl gray, flat-crowned Stetson that was set squarely on his head.

"You're going to have some company," Shanahan said, rising and standing beside his old friend.

Remington nodded. "I seen them," he said, turning his attention to the two couples waiting on the landing that fronted the station.

Shanahan ducked his head at the older pair, a tall, somber man in a dark suit who continually fingered the heavy gold watch chain looped across his flat belly, and a still-faced woman clad in a dull-colored dress and a close fitting, lace-edged bonnet. About her thin shoulders was a dark, knitted shawl.

"That there's Judge J. D. Longwell and his missus. Come in on the stage yesterday afternoon."

Remington's stolid features registered surprise. "The one they call the Hanging Judge?"

"That's him."

"Kind of far from his bailiwick, ain't he? Where the hel—where's he going?"

"Some place down Texas way. He wasn't in the notion to talk about it. I ain't sure what it's all about but I sort of got the idea he's moving permanent." Shanahan paused and jerked a thumb at the second couple.

"They's the Blackburns. Had themselves a ranch somewheres east of here. Pulling stakes, giving it up, seems, and moving back to Missouri—Independence, leastwise the husband was asking about connections to there."

"He ain't acting too happy about it," Sam observed, studying the pair.

They were young, in their mid-twenties he reckoned. The girl was slender but well built, with a calm, almost beautiful face. She was wearing a yellow skirt and jacket of soft material, a white shirtwaist cut low that fit snugly over her full bosom, and a pale-blue wool, hip-length coat —all of which struck Remington as somewhat impractical for the time and more suited to a less rigorous area.

Blackburn himself appeared to be a strong, capable man in ordinary cowhand garb, but his blocky features were downcast, serious—almost desperate . . . It was fine to be young like the Blackburns, Sam Remington thought, but he wasn't sure he'd like to go through his early years again—at least some of them. If a man could start over, and pick and choose—

"You got your bag in the boot?" Shanahan asked.

"Put it there first thing," the old driver replied.

A solitary metal suitcase, scratched and bent, it contained his extra clothing, his pistol and belt, and a leather poke in which there was about three hundred dollars. Three hundred dollars . . . Not much to show for a lifetime of work, of sitting on the seat of a wagon or high up on the box of a stagecoach—of driving horses or mules or oxen in all kinds of weather from one huddled settlement across a vast, empty land to another.

The state of his finances, however, did not bother him. He had drawn wages regularly, had seldom been without a job, and had he been of a saving nature his poke undoubtedly would be heavier, but on several occasions in the past he had sent cash to his daughter and her husband to help them over a rough spot; and that, in his estimation was the purpose of money—something to be used. He himself had never had much need for it.

Shanahan glanced to the corner of the landing. A husky young man with thick red hair, a round, open face and bold, blue eyes, had stepped into view, coming apparently from the stable and corrals behind the station. Dressed much the same as Remington, he was carrying a new whip in his hand.

"There's McElroy now," the agent said. "Reckon you'll be pulling out pretty quick. What do you think of Billy? You figure he's got the makings of a good driver?"

Remington considered his replacement dispassionately. "Ain't been around him enough to do any judging."

"According to Jeremiah's boy, Gavin, he's been handling a coach for three or four years. It was Gavin that hired him on, sent him here."

"How long he's been driving don't mean nothing. I've known some men in my time that'd been up on the box a hel—a devil of a lot longer'n that and they still didn't amount to anything. Man's got to have the feel—and that comes natural to him, or it don't."

"Meaning he never learns—"

"Oh, a fellow can learn to set up there and hold the lines and kick the brake on and off—I ain't saying he can't do that. But there's them that never do get the hang of getting the best out of a team without hurting them, or making a coach ride soft and easy instead of banging against every rock and chuckhole in the road."

"Well, I reckon Billy'll get the chance now to show what he's got—"

"He's got a mouth," Remington said acidly. "I heard him back there with the hostlers. He was telling them all about how good he was and how they'd sure better step lively when he's ready to roll. If he's half as good as he claims he is, he'll be all right."

McElroy, halted at the edge of the landing, nodded briskly to the Blackburns and the Longwells, and half-turned to look at the six-horse team being led up to the coach. He waited until the horses had been backed into position and the two hostlers were buckling and hooking up the harness, and then swaggered toward them.

Shanahan muttered under his breath: "I'd be obliged to you, Sam, if you'll sort of keep an eye on Billy. This here being his first time on the run, you can sure help him aplenty."

Remington's shoulders twitched. A stagecoach driver was like the captain of a ship. He was solely in charge and Sam had yet to meet one, including himself, that took kindly to advice when it came to handling his team and vehicle.

"That'll be up to him. He asks, I'll answer. I ain't about to stick my nose into his business without him wanting me to."

"I doubt he'll do any asking," Tom Shanahan said. "He strikes me as being plenty on the proud side."

"Nothing wrong with that long as he knows what he's about—and you told me he'd come here with some driving experience."

"All I know's what that letter from Gavin Crenshaw said . . . I sure do wish you'd change your mind about quitting."

"No chance. When I got the word Gavin was aiming to fire every driver they had that was over forty, I figured the smart thing to do was quit before he could run me off. Ain't never happened to me yet so I wasn't about to let it start."

"Funny thing about that Gavin—he ain't nothing like his pa. Never did send out no notice saying that was how things was to be; he just dropped the word and let it get rumored around. Had it been old Jeremiah we'd've all been told right straight off the shoulder. That boy sure ain't nothing like his pa."

"That's for sure."

"I'm wondering if Jeremiah knows about some of the fool things he's doing. I figure you'd be smart to hang around till he shows up and have yourself a talk with him. He's somewhere in the Territory. Been visiting the way stations and depots between here and Wichita and he's due to drop by this'n."

"It'd be a waste of time. The boy's running the outfit now and what he says goes."

"Which is sure a mighty bad thing. Hell, Gavin don't know his ass from a shotgun when it comes to the stage-line business! He'll bust this outfit in less'n a year, way he's doing things. I'll tell you this, when Jeremiah shows up here I sure aim to tell him how the cow ate the cabbage—even if it costs me my job!"

Sam Remington shook his head. "Now, don't go getting all fired up over me. I'll make out. Always have and I reckon I always will—and maybe I am getting a mite too old to do any driving—"

Shanahan spat in disgust. "You can't make me believe that, Sam—no more'n you believe it. You're just letting that little squirt Gavin push you off the box. Only thing he's interested in is the almighty dollar. Thinks he can get more work out of younger drivers and pay them less money for doing it—figures to double their runs."

"I sure wish him lots of luck," Remington said dryly, "but it ain't no sweat off'n my—ain't no business of mine any longer. Gavin Crenshaw can do what he pleases. I'm out of it."

Shanahan nodded gloomily. Back up the wide street of Apache Springs a dog was barking furiously and somewhere along the edge of the settlement a cow lowed.

Remington brushed at his sweeping mustache and rubbed at his chin. Ordinarily he wore a stubble of beard but today, his final hours in the town, he had elected to shave. Turning, he smiled briefly at the depot agent.

"I expect you got something to do besides standing here jawing with me," he said, stepping out onto the landing, "so I think I'll have me a last look around. Been nice knowing you, Tom."

"Same here," Shanahan replied. "Good luck."

2

The hostlers had hitched his favorite team to the coach. Brownie, a bay, and Prince, a chestnut, both equally slim and wiry, were the leaders. At the swing or center positions, were Dave on the near side, another bay, while his off partner, Runner, was a black. The near wheel horse was Curly, a gray, and his matching mate was a black named Dandy.

The two wheel horses, like the pair at swing, were big, strong animals built to do the work, while Brownie and Prince, lighter, consistently quicker in their responses, were naturals in the lead spots.

Moving slowly, Sam Remington approached the restless team, coming first to Dandy, the off-wheel horse. He paused there, laid a hand on the black's bowed, muscular neck, his eyes from force of habit, probing the harness, making certain there were no twisted straps, no buckles carelessly left open or snaps unsecured.

He'd miss old Dandy who had a way of pulling wide when they were rounding a bend in the road, just as he would the remaining five of the six-up. Each one of them possessed distinctive traits of some sort, a few of which were downright bad but mostly it was all show and high spirits.

Remington continued, hesitating beside the nervous horses in turn, patting a neck or a hip or gently rubbing a nose all the while murmuring words of no particular consequence at low voice. He halted after circling the leaders, reached up to scrub a smudge of dirt from one of the red glass ornaments on Dave's bridle.

He'd spent his own money decorating their harness with brass and nickel conchas and ivory rings, had personally seen to it that it was always well oiled and in perfect condition. He'd not have that pleasure any longer, Sam thought, moving on. It would be Bill McElroy's job now—assuming Billy took that much pride in his work.

Sam stopped again when he came to Curly, the near wheeler. Somehow the big gray gelding had managed to cut himself on the left foreleg. Squatting on his haunches, the old driver carefully examined the slight wound. It was superficial, scarcely more than a deep scratch—but it had not healed. Coming erect, Remington beckoned to one of the hostlers.

"Get a dab of salve and put on that cut, Otey," he said, pointing. "Ought to keep the dirt out of it."

The hostler nodded and hurried off toward the stable. Sam, giving the gray a tug at an ear, strolled on, paused once more, his narrowed eyes on the stagecoach itself.

Not as large and heavy as the Concords he'd driven back in Kansas before coming to Apache Springs, it was nevertheless similar in construction and appearance. Painted a bright red with black lettering above the door, it was a fairly new vehicle on the run, its like predecessor having been all but totally destroyed in a fire some months back.

It was an easy riding coach and one not difficult to handle. Knowingly or not, the manufacturer had copied the Concord's system of leather thorough-brace suspension, which provided a maximum of comfort for its six passengers when loaded to capacity, as well as lightening the burden of the horses. Sam Remington actually preferred it to the Concord because of its lesser weight and maneuverability but no one could ever get him to admit it was superior to the big Abbot & Downing coach.

It had been one of these lighter vehicles that had brought him his only major injury, although he could not blame it as the cause. The incident had occurred during the first years that he was on the job.

The trip to Springerville was on a regular schedule then, business having warranted a run to that distant settlement one day and a return to Apache Springs the following. Remington was making the latter when a heavy thunderstorm struck as he was descending one of Whiskey Mountain's long grades.

Lightning ripped through a pine tree that stood at the edge of the road just as the team, a different one from that headed up by Brownie and Prince, drew abreast of it. The vivid flash, the loud crackling, and explosion split the pine and sent it crashing across the road in front of the horses, causing them to veer sharply and plunge off the shoulder. A wheel struck a half-buried boulder and the coach flipped over onto its side, throwing Sam hard into a second tree.

While his two passengers were only badly shaken and the team unharmed, he sustained a broken arm and a wrenched back, both of which troubled him occasionally during wet or cold weather or when he was excessively tired.

His glance still involuntarily searching along the harness, he stepped up to the near singletree, fitted the trace loop more snugly in its hook, and stepped back. Like as not the metal would have settled itself when the horses moved out but he was no hand to leave anything to chance.

"Climb aboard, folks! We're about ready to pull out!"

Billy McElroy's voice came to Remington from the opposite side of the stagecoach. Sam quickened his step, rounded the vehicle, and glancing toward the station, nodded to Tom Shanahan. All the farewells had been said earlier and there was no point in going through them again.

Halting to allow the Blackburns and Judge Longwell and his wife to precede him into the coach, Sam put his attention on McElroy.

The young driver was taking the lines from one of the hostlers, threading those that controlled the near horses between the fingers of his left hand, gathering those of the off in his right in which he also held his new whip. Billy, feeling Remington's eyes upon him, glanced around.

"Am I doing this to suit you, mister?" he asked in a mocking tone.

Remington's stolid expression did not change. "It's you that needs pleasing, not me."

McElroy bobbed. "I'm mighty glad you said that because it sure is me that's running this outfit now. I'd like to get that straight with you."

Sam looked again toward the depot. Shanahan was still in the doorway watching, listening, as was a cowhand lounging against a corner of the building. One of the hostlers, Abe, hunkered on his heels nearby, and up in the center of the town several dogs were now barking frantically.

"Expect you're aiming to set up there on the box with me, it being where you usually ride, but that ain't how I want it. I want you inside the stage with the rest of the passengers where you belong, cause that's just what you are—a passenger and nothing else.

"I ain't heard nothing but how good a whip man you are ever since I got here, but you ain't the jehu no more—I am, and I sure don't cotton to the idea of you up there looking down your nose at me and everything I do. I make myself clear?"

"Reckon you do," Remington said quietly.

"I seen you walking around, looking things over," McElroy continued. "There was no call for you doing that. I'd done seen to it that everything was to my liking."

"There was a hook on the gray's singletree—"

"I'd seen that, too. It would've dropped into place when we started."

Remington studied the young driver thoughtfully, then finally shrugged. "Yeh, it probably would."

McElroy, the lines strung to his satisfaction, stepped up to the coach and climbed to the seat. Settling himself, he put a foot on the brake pedal and leveled his glance at Sam.

"You heard me holler all aboard, didn't you?"

"Reckon I did."

"Then climb in if you're figuring to ride with me—else stand back out of the way."

Remington pivoted slowly and moved toward the open door of the stage. He swung his attention once more to the depot. Shanahan had not stirred, nor had Abe. The cowhand, curiosity apparently satisfied, had turned away, mounted his horse, and was heading off down the south road.

Raising a hand, Sam Remington touched the brim of his hat in a final salute to the men with whom he had worked for the past decade and that he'd likely never see again, and then pulling himself into the coach, he jerked the door shut and settled on the seat beside Mrs. Blackburn.

Willie Vaughn, dark features sullen and set beneath the shadow of his wide-brimmed hat, watched as the passengers climbed into the coach—all but the old driver, Remington he'd heard him called—and took their places. But Remington didn't matter. He could be left behind for all Willie cared; it was Longwell he was interested in—Lynch Law Longwell.

He'd been hanging around Apache Springs since early morning, as well as most of the previous day, waiting. Up to then he'd been in Springerville with his older brother, Jake, and the rest of the gang scheming to hold up the bank, but then word had come from an uncle living in Jasper City where Longwell held court advising them that the judge was leaving town, and making connections, and would be on that particular Valley Stage Lines coach that specific day.

Jake had immediately suspended all plans to rob the bank. They had a family score to settle with Lynch Law Longwell and everything else must wait, for the opportunity they had hoped for had at last presented itself. Jake had immediately dispatched him, along with three of the gang, to Apache Springs where he was to keep an eye on the stage, be certain Longwell was on it, and if so, follow through with the scheme the older Vaughn, who was always good at such, had devised.

Later Jake, having some unfinished business in Springerville to take care of, would join them with the rest of their friends in the grove of cottonwoods where Lynch Law Longwell would meet the kind of justice he was so fond of handing out.

Willie listened to the words passing between Remington and the driver, a new man on the job it appeared, and wished they'd shut up and get underway. He had to cover the distance back to Three Mile Hill fast; once he was dead sure the coach with Longwell inside had pulled out, he would meet up with the rest of the men who had accompanied him—Dogie Fisk, Charlie Dodd, and Hank Skerrit—and set up the ambush.

He'd already chosen the proper place, a couple of miles this side of the hill; he couldn't afford to let anything go wrong so he had laid his plans carefully. Chances were they'd never again have as good an opportunity to square things for Lonnie, their kid brother who had ended up swinging from a hanging tree, thanks to Lynch Law Longwell.

Willie grunted in satisfaction. Remington and the driver had finished with their yammering, and lines in hand, the younger man was climbing up onto his perch. Leaning down he said something to Remington who moved off toward the coach. They were going to pull out —finally.

Drawing himself away from the side of the stage depot, Willie crossed to where his horse was tethered and stepped up into the saddle. He remained motionless, eyes on the stagecoach and its team, fiddling anxiously as they awaited the signal to move out, and then as Remington entered, found his seat, and pulled the door shut, he cut his mount around and struck for the road to Springerville. There was no need to delay any longer.

Behind him he heard the shout of the driver, the sudden ring of harness metal, the quick thud of hoofs as the man on the box popped his whip. He knew without looking back that the hostler who had been holding to the bridle of one of the leader horses had released his grip and stepped clear, and that the stage was rolling.

The long wait at last was over, Willie Vaughn realized. All the months of hoping for the right opportunity to even the score with Lynch Law Longwell was at hand—no more than a few hours away. He was going to enjoy every minute of the trial and execution.

3

The coach rocked back on its leather springs as the horses lunged into their harness, dipped forward, and leveled off. The houses of Apache Springs whipped past in a blur and shortly they were out of the settlement and racing swiftly along the road leading south.

The Longwells were on the front seat, riding backward. Facing them were the Blackburns, the man next to the window, his wife in the center, while Sam Remington occupied a position at the opposite opening. Longwell was staring disinterestedly out at the fleeting landscape, his eyes distant and likely seeing none of it. His wife, her shawl now low about her shoulders was lost in contemplation of her high button shoes.

The Blackburns were equally detached, he also silently viewing the countryside, she idly plucking at the folds of her skirt. The woman was much younger and even prettier than he'd thought, Remington realized, studying her covertly, and wondered just what the trouble was between the two. But it was something he'd likely never be made aware of; folks ordinarily didn't air their problems before strangers, and no decent man would have the gall to intrude by asking.

The Longwells were no better off, seeming as far apart as two total strangers. Sam speculated on the possibility that they were not getting along—and he reckoned that could be the problem with the Blackburns as well, but of course it could be something entirely different; outside pressures often weighed heavily upon a couple and drove a wedge between them.

He'd heard reports of J. D. Longwell and the iron-handed court where he sat in judgment on malefactors. It was well known that he was more than generous with the death penalty—a fact that earned him the slurring nicknames bandied about in that part of the Territory where he occupied the bench.

Whatever it was, it was none of his business, Remington assured himself. In all probability both couples would eventually work it all out to their mutual satisfaction.

"Hey—ooo, Brownie! Prince! Ho, Runner—Dave! Curly—Dandy! Get along, get along!"

Billy McElroy's voice floated back faintly above the thudding of the horses' hoofs and the whir and grind of iron-tired wheels cutting into the gritty soil. Churning dust boiled past the stage in a thick, tan cloud, part of which swept by the speeding coach to create a pursuing pall, and part whipped through the windows and into the vehicle where it hung like a restless, spinning curtain between the passengers.

Despite the fact he'd been over the route countless times Sam Remington had never really had a good look at the country. Absorbed in driving, his impression had been one of trees, rocks, bluffs, grassy meadows, and hills caught from the corner of an eye as they flashed by. None of it had taken precise shape or definite character and, on the whole, the beauty of it was lost to him.

But on this, his final passage, he was being afforded the

opportunity of seeing the world that had been his as it was—fresh and vivid now with the pulsing regeneration of spring.

The road, he saw, cut straight and true along the floor of a broad valley in the particular area, and where the land fell away at either side to sweep gracefully upward and meet the rise of distant hills, the grass had thickened to cover the scars of winter with rich green while patches of red and yellow flowers were often visible.

Cottonwoods, here in singles, there in various size groves, were already fully leafed, and the sturdy cedars and junipers that dared grow on the steeper grades were a deep emerald. In the sandy washes he could see stands of grayish rabbitbush and Apache plume; thistle and bayonet yucca were plentiful on the more barren ground, while scattered chollas, thorny fingers only weeks previous drooping under the stress of cold weather, were now rigidly erect, patiently awaiting the unwary passer-by.

It was all there and he had borne witness to none of it—the carpet of grass, the bright flowers, the frowning, rugged formations of granite and sandstone, the trees and the majestic hills. He'd missed it all, Sam Remington thought ruefully.

To him it had been a matter of seasons, of spring when the rains struck and the road became a treacherous sea of mud; summer, with the heat setting in and doubling the work of the horses, of fall and the mornings and evenings razor sharp and warning that bitter weather would soon arrive; and then winter with its numbing winds and freezing snow and sleet that turned a man's blood to ice. Of those changing factors he had been constantly aware, and such being true, he reckoned he had not missed out entirely for in just passing through he had been a part of it.

Sam, feeling a light touch on his knee, faced Mrs. Blackburn. Her lovely features were quiet, solemn.

"Do you know what time we'll get to Springerville?"

"About four o'clock, ma'am," Remington replied.

The stage, rushing onto a rough stretch in the road, suddenly began to creak and pop noisily as it rocked and jolted across the uneven surface. It was over as abruptly as it had begun, and when they were again rolling along smoothly the girl resumed.

"Isn't there a stop in between somewhere—a place where we'll take lunch?"

"Yes, ma'am—Halverson's way station. Ought to get there around noon. It'll be an hour layover. We eat and change teams there."

"Thank you," Mrs. Blackburn said quietly and lapsed into silence.

"That the only stop?" Longwell asked, rousing.

"It's the only way station, if that's what you mean. This here's a short, kind of easy run. Only seventy mile."

"Most stage lines change horses oftener than that—"

Remington shrugged at the faintly critical observation. "Yeh, I know. A team usually runs twenty-five, maybe thirty miles. But like I said, this here is an easy run except for a couple of hills. Most all of it's on the flat—and we've got a six-up pulling the coach. Ain't no need for more'n one change."

The judge dropped his head, returned to his previous morose state. His wife shifted, adjusted her shawl and brushed at her pinched face with a lace-edged handkerchief. A fine film of yellowish dust now covered them all.

"Hey—Runner! Dave—"

McElroy's shout was punctuated by the pistol-like crack of his whip. Remington frowned, clawed at his beardless chin. Billy's yelling at the horses was all right and to be expected—but using the whip was uncalled for. The horses knew the road, its rises and falls, its twists and turns; they didn't need to be reminded that a grade was ahead or that a stretch of loose sand was to be crossed at no break in speed. McElroy had only to leave it up to Prince and Brownie, the leaders.

But that now was of no concern to him—or shouldn't be. By this time next week he'd be in Santa Fe and comfortably settled with his daughter and her family. The farthest thing from his mind ought to be the road lying between Apache Springs and Springerville and the stagecoach that plied it.

He hoped he could adjust to the way of life he was entering, hoped also that he could find something with which to fill the days that stretched ahead. He wasn't so damned old, he'd told himself several times—fifty or thereabouts, he wasn't exactly sure—even if he always did feel ancient when he was around people like the Blackburns and Billy McElroy. Somehow they made him *feel* old, just as did the aches and pains that beset him on cold days.

He'd try for a job around a livery stable or maybe even a stage depot—one where he could be around horses. Of course he could expect his daughter to object to his becoming a stableboy, and he had no wish to be shoveling manure out of stalls and doing similar chores, but she shouldn't oppose his desire to work with horses, keeping them fit and such.

He'd given the thought of retirement a lot of consideration; he had wondered if he'd be able to take it, and reckoned he would. A man could adjust to about anything once he made up his mind, but finding a job of the sort he was thinking of sure would make it all go down easier. He wished Jeremiah Crenshaw and the Valley Stage Lines company had a place in Santa Fe. Like as not he'd be able to swing a job with them—but even if he didn't he'd get the chance to be around Brownie and Prince and all the other horses he'd known and considered his friends for those past years.

The coach began to slow, McElroy's strident voice now becoming more pronounced as the pounding of the team and the creaking of the coach decreased.

Mrs. Blackburn sat up straight, a puzzled look on her face as she glanced at Sam Remington.

"Is this the way station—Halverson's—already? It doesn't seem like we've gone—"

"Not Halverson's—just a stop to blow the horses. They've pulled a long grade and we always call a halt here at the top to give them a few minutes' rest."

The stage had come to a dead stop, and as the dust swirling about it began to settle, McElroy's voice cut through the pall.

"Everybody out! Chance to stretch your legs, folks."

Remington reached for the door handle. Releasing the lock he stepped out, and turning, assisted Mrs. Blackburn and then Mrs. Longwell to dismount.

"Aim to be here about fifteen, twenty minutes," McElroy continued, coming off the box. "Any of you got to do your duty, best you don't go wandering too far off in the woods—leastwise no farther'n it takes to get out of sight."

Mrs. Blackburn blushed and the judge's wife looked away to conceal her embarrassment. Remington stared at the young driver for a long moment and moved off. Billy McElroy needed to be taught some manners.

4

Sam Remington strolled leisurely to the edge of the small flat upon which McElroy had halted the stage. It was a short distance off the road and from there he could look back down into the valley across which they had just traveled. The brown scar of the trail was a narrow, almost perfectly straight line, running due north.

Wheeling lazily he saw that Billy McElroy, as any good driver should, was checking his team and their harness. The Longwells were standing off to one side, aloof and unhappy while the Blackburns were walking, an arm's length apart, back toward the road.

Overhead several crows were straggling through the steel-blue sky, and somewhere down the slope where there was a prairie dog village one of the small animals was barking a warning to others of his kind. Evidently there was a coyote close by, or it could be a hawk or some other swift-striking predator. The price of life for the small tan and white rodents was constant vigilance as they counted enemies at every hand.

"No, Stacey—wait—"

Blackburn's strained plea drew Sam's attention and brought him around. The girl was walking hurriedly down the road. Her husband was close behind her, hand outstretched. He caught up and grasped her by the arm. She pulled free, began to run. Blackburn followed. In a half a dozen strides he again overtook her, seized her wrist, and brought her to a halt.

For a long minute they stood there, face to face with the man speaking earnestly and rapidly, his lean features serious. Finally the girl shrugged, and with her husband still holding firmly to her arm, they turned and started back in the direction of the stagecoach.

Remington, seeing both glance at him and unwilling to further embarrass them, turned away. He hesitated as they veered, bending their steps toward him. The girl, he noticed, appeared somewhat reluctant.

"Mister," Blackburn called.

Frowning, Sam said: "Name's Remington."

"Can we talk to you for a bit?"

The old driver pushed his hat to the back of his head, looked to the direction of the Longwells. They were watching curiously. McElroy was somewhere on the far side of the team.

"Sure—"

The couple had halted before him. Both were flushed, either from anger or exertion, Sam had no way of knowing which.

"I'm Travis Blackburn. This here's my wife, Stacey."

Remington acknowledged the belated introduction. Then, "What's on your mind?"

"It's sort of hard talking to a stranger about the kind of troubles we've got," Travis Blackburn said, the words pouring out in a rush as if he feared to lose courage and must speak before such occurred, "but you were real nice and friendly to my wife back down the road a ways—and we just got to hash things out with somebody. You being older, I figured you'd probably know about these things, could talk to my wife, make her understand—advise her. We ain't got no folks around here."

Remington smiled wryly, shook his head. "I never was no great shakes at passing out advice—"

"We're breaking up," Blackburn plunged on heedlessly, "and heading back home to Missouri, leastwise Stacey is. I've tried to talk her out of it, make her see that things are bound to change but she won't listen. You know what she was doing running off down the road there a minute or so ago?"

"I was going to walk to that way station," Stacey Blackburn said firmly before Remington could make a reply. "I can't—I won't listen to Travis's begging any longer. The instant we got out of the stagecoach he started in again."

"You won't listen to reason, that's what's wrong!" Travis declared. "You know I'm right but you're too stubborn to see things my way."

"Your way—that's the trouble! It's always your way!" Tears glistened in the girl's eyes.

Remington raised both hands. Palms forward, he waved the Blackburns into silence. "Now, you asked me to do some listening. All right, I will, but you're both going to have to ease up a mite. I can't make heads or tails of what this here's all about. And you," he added, looking directly at the girl, "best forget about walking to Halverson's way station from here. It's a far piece—a far piece in fact to anywhere from the top of this hill."

McElroy was doing something with Runner's belly-band, making an adjustment probably. The horses were quieting down, making the most of the respite. Judge and Mrs. Longwell had turned away, viewing the distant hills and the intervening valley.

"How long you two been hitc—married?" Sam asked, coming back to the Blackburns. As long as he was being sucked into a family argument he'd best start at the beginning.

"Two years last month," Travis said.

"You said you came from Missouri—"

"Independence."

"Where've you been living? I don't recollect ever seeing either one of you around Apache Springs before this morning."

"We've got a place up near Stoker—about a hundred miles on east. Cattle country."

"You raising cattle?"

"That's what I'm hoping to do," Travis said heavily. "My pa gave Stacey and me a little ranch he got his hands on a time ago, for a wedding present. We moved onto it right off, but the going's been hard and we haven't been able to do much—"

"Much!" Stacey echoed bitterly. Her color was high and her blue eyes now sparked. "We haven't been able to do anything with it! It's practically the same as it was the day we got there—dirty, cold, no better than living in a—"

"Are you claiming I haven't tried to fix things up, make it better and easier for you?"

Stacey bit at her lower lip. "No, Travis, I'm not. You've tried. I'll admit that but you just haven't been able to accomplish anything."

"It's not my fault we lost what few head of stock we had that first winter. You can't blame me because it was the worst storm that had hit the country in years."

"I know that and I'm not blaming you. It's just that everything's against us—the weather, the country, even the people it seems. And there never was any money—barely enough to buy things to eat."

"You could've looked after that garden we planted—"

"How was I to know the crows and the gophers, or whatever they were, would eat up everything as fast as it came out of the ground? I couldn't sit out there day and night keeping watch—and with you gone all the time I never—"

"Gone?" Remington cut in, puzzled.

Travis Blackburn rubbed nervously at his jaw. "When we lost our start I had to get out and find work. Done odd jobs for other ranchers—mending fences, fixing wagons—things their regular cowhands wouldn't do."

"We could have moved into some town where you might have found a regular job," Stacey said coldly.

"What town? There wasn't none around big enough for merchants to hire help. They all run their stores themselves."

"I expect you would have run into something. Anyway, anything would have been better than the way it was," the girl said and leveled her attention on Remington. "Sometimes he'd be gone for days and I'd be alone in that shack, afraid to step outside for fear some of those tramps—drifters would see me as they were riding by, and stop—"

"I tried to make it home every night but now and then I was working some place that was just too far away to manage it—and there were a few times when I was just too damned tired after putting in twelve or fourteen hours at hard labor. I done the best I could, Stacey, but I ain't sure you did."

"What more could you ask of me?" the girl demanded. "I was there, waiting, and I did everything I could with what little we had."

"*What little we had!* You've rubbed that into me a hundred times in the last couple of months!"

"It's the truth, no matter the reason or the cause, but it's neither here nor there now, Travis. I'm finished."

Blackburn turned imploringly to Sam Remington. "You see? There's just no reasoning with her. I've tried over and over but all I get is how bad things were thrown up to me every other breath. I keep telling her it'll all change, that bad luck can't last forever—"

"There's no guarantee of that," Stacey said. "Not even a small promise."

"Things just can't go on like they have. There's always a change for the better when they're on the bottom. They can't do anything but go up."

"Don't go quoting me any of those old saws," the girl said, shaking her head. "I've listened to too many of them and none of them ever proved to be true. I'm going home, Travis. Nothing can make me change my mind."

"If you'd only listen—try—"

"If you like you can forget taking me all the way back to Independence. You can drop off at Halverson's, or whatever the name of that way station is, and go on back to your ranch . . . I—I don't want to ever see it again."

Travis Blackburn muttered under his breath, shifted his attention to Sam.

"Reckon you see now what the trouble is."

Remington nodded. "Yeh, sure can. Now, I've been a long time in single harness, my wife having died near thirty year ago, but I remember that getting along was a little more than a fifty-fifty deal like some folks claim.

"I was gone a lot of the time, too, skinning freight for first one outfit and then another, or driving stagecoachs for some company, and I reckon we had pretty much the same problems you two are having.

"I was working hard—we had us a baby the first year we was married—and times being what they was, it took a lot of doing to just put grub on the table and come up with the other things a family needs.

"But I sort of kept remembering that it was me that was out and getting around while my wife was having to stay home and see to the baby and look after all the rest of what little we had—which sure wasn't much, I can tell you. Place we had sounds a whole lot like the one you folks've been living in—four walls and a roof and not much else—"

"But you stayed together, didn't you?" Travis cut in. "Your wife stuck it out—"

"Well, yes, she did, but I don't think she would've if I hadn't gone out of my way to make things a bit easier for her. I seen to it that the neighbors—we only had a couple—dropped by while I was gone. And I made arrangements with the fellow that run the store in town—we lived about ten mile away—so's she could get whatever she wanted on credit."

"I won't have credit!" Blackburn said flatly. "My pa says—"

"I even done some trading around and got a buggy and a little mare to pull it so's she'd have something to go visiting in herself. I recollect I had to work a couple a evenings every week for dang nigh a year to pay for that rig—but it was sure worth it.

"The point I'm trying to make, Blackburn, is that a man can't think of a marriage being that fifty-fifty split. A man can put up with most anything, no matter how tough going it is, but a woman, being a woman, needs more, and I figure it's up to a fellow to see that she gets it. Now, I'd say a good arrangement would be more like seventy-thirty with the husband being on the seventy side and expecting no more than thirty from his wife.

"Out here a woman is a mighty precious thing to my way of thinking, and there ain't no shame in a man bending over backwards caring for her."

5

A silence followed Sam Remington's words, one broken only by a camp-robber jay scolding noisily in a nearby cedar. Finally Stacey Blackburn spoke.

"It's too late, even if—"

"It's up to the wife to give a little, same as the husband," Travis muttered.

"Not saying it ain't," Remington agreed, "but life's hard on a woman out here, makes them old before their time."

"Ain't no easy cinch for a man either. You've got to admit, Stacey, that I didn't back off of work."

The girl shrugged, gazing toward the distant hills. Down at the foot of the slope the prairie dog, the same or another, broke into a staccato run of barking again.

"Wife's supposed to stand by her husband even when things go bad," Blackburn continued. "You promised to in the marriage ceremony, swore you'd—"

"I know what my vows were," the girl interrupted coolly. "And I remember yours. Perhaps I haven't lived up to mine fully, but can you say you have yours?"

Sam Remington stirred restlessly and swore under his breath. He was ill at ease and half angry at being thrust into the center of a family problem involving a couple with whom he had no connection and did not know up until that hour, but they had turned to him for help and he would not put his back to them.

"Now, hold on," he said gently. "You two are doing nothing more'n wrangling, and they ain't going to get you nowheres. What's done's done. There ain't nothing gained in hashing it over and over. What you need to figure out is what each of you wants and try to strike a bargain somewheres in between—that is, if you aim to stay married." He paused, placing his eyes on the girl. "You want that?"

"What I don't want is a life of being dirt poor and lonely and slaving away in a shack at the end of nowhere —with nothing in sight but—"

"That's not what I asked," Remington broke in. "You want to keep your marriage going or don't you? Now, if you don't there ain't no use in us wasting breath."

Stacey looked down, her face drawn into tight lines that all but destroyed its beauty. "Of course I want it to last, but unless—"

"How about you?" Sam asked, shifting his attention to Travis Blackburn.

"You know damn well I do! I wouldn't be trying to talk her out of leaving me if I didn't!"

"Then both of you best straighten out your thinking and your wanting and find out what it'll take to keep you together."

"I just want to live a decent, normal life—like other people," Stacey said at once. "I want a home and nice furniture and pictures on the wall—and children. And I want a husband that I know will be home every night."

"And what I want, and aim to have, is my own ranch where I can raise cattle and amount to something before I get too old to do it."

"Even if it costs you your wife?" Sam said quietly.

Travis shrugged helplessly. "No—I don't mean—"

"It's sure what you're saying. Best you sort out your meanings and get them straight. And you, missy, that fine, high-toned way of living you're hankering for, any chance of you settling for a bit less—leastwise for a while?"

Stacey shook her head. "I've already put in two years of settling for less. I think it's only right that he see it my way now."

"Be a clerk in some store, selling groceries and dry goods and things like that?" Travis shouted. "No, sir—I won't listen to that kind of a deal!"

Remington sighed and glanced toward the team and Billy McElroy. It was about time to pull out and resume the run to Halverson's; it couldn't come too soon.

"Ain't sure what to say now," he said slowly. "I just—"

"Didn't you and your wife ever have any differences? Wasn't you ever faced with a problem like mine—ours?" Blackburn persisted.

"Sure. I doubt if there's a couple that ever lived that didn't have problems—but most of them had enough savvy to set down and work them out and not just blow up like a two-dollar pistol and quit.

"Something you both ought to get in your minds: don't ever give up on anything that's worth something to you. There's always an answer somewhere if you'll keep looking—and trying."

"I am trying!" Travis said in a desperate voice. It was not yet warm but beads of sweat were gathered on his forehead. "It's not getting me anywhere—and you sure ain't being much help."

Remington stiffened, a sharp reminder that he had not asked to be cast in the role of mediator springing to his lips, but he let it die. Travis likely didn't mean it the way it sounded.

"I told you right off at the start I wasn't no hand at this kind of thing. I only recollect what me and my wife done when we found ourselves barking back and forth and there didn't look like there was a way out."

"What was that?"

"Already told you—I done the bending, the giving in. My wife then'd sort of do the same, and we'd wind up somewheres on middle ground."

Sam's words were mostly fiction. There had been few problems of a serious nature arising between him and Patience Remington. She had been a strong, dauntless woman capable of coping with any situation. She mastered early poverty, loneliness, and grief with a straightforward, head-held-high attitude and made the best of life whether it was favoring or had turned upon them. As near as he could recall she had never once complained during the years they were married. . . . But it was only a small, white lie, one he felt might serve a good purpose.

"I'm thinking maybe you're both right and you're both wrong," Remington said, and put his glance on Stacey. "Could be you're trying to walk before you can crawl, missy. Most folks don't get a fine home with all the fixings until they've worked and lived a spell.

"And being a big rancher, Blackburn—that takes a powerful long time unless you've got a pocketful of gold to start with—which you ain't. Now, you've got the land and just letting it lay there ain't going to hurt it none.

"Why don't you move into some town, get yourself a job and start saving money so's you can someday have that ranch you're wanting. Meantime you'll be making your wife happy and giving her what she wants. Ain't that so, missy?"

Stacey nodded soberly. "It doesn't have to be a big, fine house—just a decent place to live, one where I could feel safe and know that—"

"It's all right for me to give up what I want to do as long as you get what you want, that it?" Travis snapped angrily. "I have to settle for a two-bit job selling spools of thread to old ladies or something like that so's you can have a house. Well, I—"

"Be only for as long as it'd take you to save up enough cash—"

"Which could be years—my whole lifetime, maybe!"

Remington's patience was rapidly running dry. He studied Blackburn thoughtfully. "Reckon that boils it down right there to what means the most to you—your wife or your wantings. Seems to me that's the problem and you're going to have to make the choice."

Travis shook his head. "Ain't fair, putting it all up to me. I—"

"Climb aboard, folks!"

Billy McElroy's shout cut into Blackburn's anguished complaint. Immediately Stacey pivoted and started for the coach. Sam smiled tightly at Travis.

"Nobody ever said life was fair, or easy. A man gets out of it what he puts into it, and the less he puts into it the harder things go for him. . . . Come on, we best get on our seats. That driver's as apt to leave us standing here as not."

Squatting on his heels, back against a tall pine, Willie Vaughn maintained his steady vigilance on the crown of a distant rise. The stagecoach would first appear there, and when it did it would be time to move out.

"They ought to be showing up—"

It was the second time in five minutes that Hank Skerrit had made his impatient observation. Willie turned to him and considered the man—dark, round faced, about his own age and with a neatly cropped mustache in which he took extraordinary pride.

"Ain't nobody holding you here, Hank. If you're in such an all-fired hurry to go somewheres, why, go right ahead. Expect me and Charlie and Dogie can handle this."

Skerrit mumbled a curse, then shrugged. "I ain't wanting to go nowheres. Just that this here setting around waiting gives me the jumps."

"Who all's on that coach?" Dogie Fisk asked, breaking the slight tension that had risen.

"The judge and his woman. Some hayshaker and his. And Sam Remington."

"Who the hell's Sam Remington?"

"A driver for the stage outfit. He's quit and moving—to Santa Fe I think it was. Heard them all talking about it while I was standing around making sure old Lynch Law'd be aboard."

"There ain't no shotgun rider?"

"Nope. Never ride one—leastwise they haven't in a long time. Stage don't carry nothing but passengers and dang few of them. It's not worth holding up."

Fisk, an angular blond with narrow, hard-set features, spat into the loose gravel. "Ought to be easy doings. Ain't nobody we got to worry about but the driver."

"He packing iron?" Charlie Dodd wondered. Dodd was the eldest of the four, barely thirty.

Willie nodded. "Wearing a six-gun. I don't know if he can use it. It may be only for show."

Skerrit rose and walked about restlessly. "Well, I hope we can make this short. I hated giving up on that bank and the sooner we get back to it, the better I'll be liking it. . . . You sure Jake and the rest of the boys'll be here?"

"I'm sure," Willie said laconically.

"When was they aiming to leave Springerville?"

"Last night—or maybe early this morning. Don't fret none about Jake and them. They'll be here on time."

"But what if they ain't? We going ahead with what you and him want to do?"

"We wait for Jake—that's what we'll do."

"But maybe him and the boys'll get hung up. We just can't set there in that grove and twiddle our thumbs. Somebody's sure to come looking for that stage when it don't show up at that way station."

"Ain't likely. This ain't no regular run any more—it just sort of makes the trip when there's passengers needing hauling. We can figure there ain't nobody expecting it—not for a couple of days, anyway. . . . And quit your stewing. Jake'll be here. He wants this bad as I do—maybe even more. Lonnie was sort of special to him."

"Well, I'd sure feel a hell of a lot easier if he was already here," Skerrit muttered, again hunching on his heels. "I don't see why he couldn't've come with us in the first place."

"He had business to take care of—"

"Business! Expect that red-headed woman he's been messing around with is the business he had to take care of."

"Maybe so," Willie Vaughn said coolly. "When he gets here why don't you ask him?"

Skerrit reached into a pocket in his vest and drew out

his cigarette makings. "No, I reckon not," he drawled, rolling himself a smoke. "It ain't that important to me."

Willie laughed. "I didn't figure it would be. . . . Now, I don't want none of you to forget what I said about shooting. It comes down to using guns, be goddammed careful you don't hit the judge. We want him alive. The rest don't matter. Savvy?"

Dogie Fisk bobbed. "Reckon we do—you sure told us often enough."

Vaughn's mouth was a grim line. "All right—just don't make no mistake."

6

Twenty years on the bench, actually thirty serving the law if you counted the time when he was a practicing attorney. Now it was all down the river. Gone—lost. And for what?

John Davis Longwell swore softly in deep frustration. For nothing—nothing more than the knowledge that he was a hated, despised man, reviled from all sides, considered to be no less a killer than the criminals to whom he had meted out justice.

He'd borne the burden of that realization for longer than he'd like to admit believing it was his duty, part and parcel, in fact, of the responsibility he had accepted. But finally it had all grown too heavy. He'd found himself wondering, doubting, questioning his position in the scheme of things. Was he what everyone seemed to believe—a cold-blooded, heartless man devoid of feeling, using his exalted, all-powerful status as a judge to satisfy his subconscious blood lust?

Had he abandoned the oath he'd sworn to obey, that of holding sacred the law, upholding it and administering justice fairly and impartially? How could he tell? He didn't think so, but he could be too close to it—and there was never anyone he could talk to about it.

Sophie meant well but hers was a small, narrow world in which she confined herself totally. There had been a time ten—no it was more like fifteen years ago—when she was active socially, had women friends, went to church functions and participated in various civic affairs.

But that had all come to an end; as his reputation had grown and the vicious sobriquets of *Lynch Law Longwell* and the *Hanging Judge* became common expressions along the streets, Sophie had gradually withdrawn from life, turned from a smiling, if pompous woman to little more than a recluse, refusing to leave the seclusion of their home.

He'd tried even as far back as then to determine what, if any, truth lay in the implications of those abominable terms, but search his mind and soul as he would he could find no satisfactory answer. And so it had rocked along day by day, week by week, month into month until it became years. All that time he had faithfully adhered to his task of upholding the letter of the law according to his interpretation, and striving all the while to ignore the slanderous tales and spiteful titles applied to him.

At last he'd surrendered to conscience and indecision. He resolved to resign, move, go far away where the name of John Davis Longwell was unknown, and resume the practice of law. Let someone else make the decision of life or death over the accused.

He was failing himself and the law. He knew that and it was a thorn pricking him in the side. But he was a man weary of battling the world and his own self over what was right and what was wrong. He longed for nights when he could sleep as other men did—without conscience plaguing him with its sullen, persistent voice.

He looked forward to the day when he could walk down a street and find a friendly face and not see only repugnance and scowls of hate, and overhear murmured epithets and words of contempt.

That day was not far off. Those few who hypocritically upheld him as a judge but shunned him as a man, the others who openly or secretly decried his methods—let them find another man to stand between them and the outlaw world. Let them call him quitter, coward, and other derogatory names—they didn't know what it was like to live under the conditions he'd known, to be the object of scorn by the law-abiding, of pure hatred by the lawless. He was done with it.

Longwell turned, leveled his emotionless eyes at the young couple conversing so earnestly with Remington, the stagecoach driver he'd heard the agent at the depot say was retiring from his job.

He didn't believe the couple was acquainted with Remington; they hadn't acted so during the ride up from Apache Springs. Evidently they had simply taken whatever problem they were having to him, using him as a sounding board.

Young people could do that—walk up to a perfect stranger, particularly if he was older—and enlist his aid. When a man got up in years, as he was, it was out of the question. It was pride, he supposed, that forbade it.

Longwell frowned and turned as he heard the stage driver sing out. Maybe he'd feel better about it all if he swallowed some of his pride and talked things over with Sam Remington—or even with the young couple. He'd wanted to do just that years ago but there'd never been anyone around he could turn to—or trust. Now, here, among total strangers, maybe he could find some answers.

Reaching out he took his wife by the arm. "Come, Sophie," he said, "it's time to go," and started for the coach.

Billy McElroy set the brake on the stagecoach, secured the lines, and calling out his instructions to the passengers, climbed down from the seat. At once he moved to the front of the team, halted beside the off leader and began to fiddle with the harness. He was trembling slightly and he didn't want anyone, particularly Sam Remington, to become aware of it.

The first leg of the run had gone well, he believed, and he was damned glad he'd ordered Remington to ride inside the coach with the rest of the customers where no note of his mistakes, should he make any, would be seen.

He'd bluffed, even lied a bit to get the job, knowing full well he lacked the qualifications to handle a six-horse hitch team and a coach full of passengers. But he had been able to convince the man who bossed the Valley Stage outfit—a fellow not much older than himself—that he was, and after that, despite the fact that he realized the danger he'd be exposing all those who rode with him to, there was no backing out.

Actually his experience consisted of no more than driving farm wagons although once, for a short distance, he'd been allowed to take the reins of a four-up drawing an ore wagon. He'd failed at that—cutting too short and getting his team all tangled up in their harness.

But that hadn't cooled his desire to become a stagecoach driver. There was something inside him that demanded he attain that peak of prestige and glory, and that he do so by whatever means necessary—and requirements be damned.

Luck had favored him. He got word the Valley Lines needed a driver in a hurry. He'd hunted up the boss, persuaded him that he was the man for the job, and gotten himself hired.

From then on there was nothing left to do but bull his

way on through by calling on memory for the things he'd seen drivers do and give the impression to others that he was a regular hand at it. He'd managed to augment his knowledge considerably by hanging around Apache Springs for a few days before taking over during which time he got the hostlers and grooms in conversation, bragging a great deal about imaginary exploits of the past while slyly slipping in questions every now and then that had to do with the job.

It was a fairly easy drive, he'd learned. The road followed level ground through the Whiskey Mountains most of the way. There were only a couple of hills and the summits of those attained by long, gentle grades in which there were no sharp bends. It should be a cinch. All he need do was sit up there on the box, let the horses run free and do the work. Hell, by the time he reached Springerville he'd truly have the experience everybody thought was so necessary—and he'd finally be an honest-to-God stagecoach driver.

He wished there was some way the folks back in Arkansas could be made aware of that fact. Maybe there'd be a picture gallery in Springerville. If so, he'd get one made of him sitting high up there on the seat of the stage, holding the lines of the six-horse team, and send it back to his folks.

They'd fair bust with pride and be showing it to people all the way from Hank's Crossing to Parkerstown, and maybe it would put a stop to that smart-alec bunch making fun of him the way they were always doing. They'd pure have to respect him once they saw the proof that he was a stagecoach driver.

Billy, the nervous quivering of his leg muscles finally over, threw a covert glance at Sam Remington. The old driver was busy talking to that young couple—jeez, what a looker she was—and the judge and his wife were taking in the view of the valley from the crest of the hill.

He reckoned they were all going to keep their distance—not that it mattered now because he'd settled down; he was steady as a rock. He guessed he ought to look things over the way he'd noticed other drivers do; examine the harness, make a show of inspecting the horses and the coach. It didn't make a lot of sense—that was the job of the hostlers and they were supposed to do it before the coach pulled out, but he supposed he'd as well get himself in the habit. Folks seemed to expect it.

Billy moved on, going from horse to horse, fingering the straps, the bellybands, shaking the collars and hames as if to be certain all fit properly. He had a close look at the wheels of the coach, made sure the boot straps were buckled, came finally at a halt again at the shoulder of Prince, the off leader. He'd made the rounds. Anybody watching ought to be satisfied.

Reaching down, he adjusted the pistol hanging at his hip, bringing it forward where it would be more comfortable, and then taking out the gold watch he'd more or less borrowed from a drunk back in Kansas, he consulted its Roman numerals. It was time to go—past time, in fact. Wheeling to his passengers, Billy started to mount to the box.

"Climb aboard, folks!" he called in his most authoritative voice.

7

Remington, the last to enter the coach, was barely seated when the stage lurched forward into motion, cut sharp left and regained the road. Billy McElroy's voice became a constant sound as he shouted at the horses and several times the popping of his whip could be heard.

Sam shook his head, settled back, and made himself comfortable for the remainder of the ride to Halverson's. Driver Billy McElroy had best take care; the grade they were slanting onto from the crest of the rise was lengthy, if not too steep, and the team given too much encouragement, would sure as hell overrun itself.

"Forget that yelling and that damned whip," Remington muttered to himself.

"You say something?" Longwell asked, leaning forward as the stagecoach continued to gather speed.

"Only to myself," Sam replied and swore again as the coach began to sway.

The judge, one hand gripping the sill of the window beside which he sat, frowned deeply. "Aren't we going a bit fast for this slope?"

Remington, company interests paramount from force of long habit, managed a smile. "Expect he's just getting underway. Be fine in a couple of minutes. No danger."

But there was. If that fool McElroy didn't start pulling in the team they'd like as not end up in the ditch plenty soon, he thought, and entertained the idea of leaning out the door and yelling a few choice words pertaining to caution at the young driver.

In the next moment he felt headlong speed of the stage slacken, the creaking and erratic swaying cease. McElroy had evidently realized he was tempting fate and put himself to slowing the horses.

"I understand you used to drive this coach," Longwell said. He had relaxed somewhat, sitting with his shoulders against the back of the seat, and his fingers no longer locked tight to the edge of the window.

"Ten year, more or less," Sam said, nodding.

"And now you're retiring—"

Again Remington bobbed. "Aim to spend the rest of my days in Santa Fe—living with my daughter."

"It's nice having a family to go to. Mrs. Longwell and I never had any children," the judge said, and then added: "You don't appear to be a man ready to retire."

"That was the company's idea, not mine."

"I see—I beg your pardon. I neglected to introduce myself and my wife . . . I'm Judge J. D. Longwell . . . my wife, Sophie."

"I've heard of you," Sam said, extending his arm, and watched something close down in the man's eyes as if he expected some comment made relating to his identity.

Remington, clasping the judge's lean fingers in his own, said no more but nodded politely to Sophie Longwell and then ducked his head at the younger couple.

"These folks are the Blackwells, in case you haven't met. She's Stacey and he's Travis."

The round of introductory ritual was repeated, the brief handshakes, the quiet murmurs of acknowledgment.

Beyond the curving confines of the stagecoach the thudding of hoofs and the whirring of wheels laid a rhythmic background to it all.

"We're going to Texas," Longwell stated in a tentative voice. He seemed anxious to start a conversation. "I expect to resume my law practice there."

Remington's brows lifted in surprise. "You quitting being a judge? Always figured that was sort of a lifetime job."

"It generally is," Longwell replied; he hesitated as his wife placed her hand upon his, pressing it warningly. He drew away, shrugged, lowered his head. "The truth is I couldn't stand—couldn't continue to administer the office as I should."

A long pause followed the barely audible words. Remington finally broke the hush.

"Never heard of a judge just up and quitting."

"You have now. Let someone else sit in my chair and deal with the lawbreakers. I've had enough."

Travis Blackburn stirred. "Expect that could get to be a mighty sorrowful thing—sending men to their deaths or maybe to spend the rest of their lives in a prison. Would kind of hang on my mind was it me having to do it."

"The law has to be upheld," Longwell said, rising to the defense of his profession. "Without it we'd be living like animals in the woods."

Remington was studying the jurist closely. That Longwell wasn't happy with his intended future was clear, yet there was a resoluteness about him that said there would be no turning back.

"Folks owe men like you a big debt—putting killers and such away where they can't hurt anybody," he said.

J. D. Longwell's smile was bitter. "Too few people ever realize that, and even then most have little respect for us.

They look upon my kind much as they do a hangman—a necessary evil but someone to avoid and ridicule with vile nicknames and slurring remarks."

"That the reason you're quitting?" Remington asked bluntly.

Longwell shifted uncomfortably on his seat. The Blackburns had lost interest, were immersed in self thoughts. Sophie Longwell, her cold, transparent features grim set, was staring straight ahead, eyes fixed on the wall of the coach behind the young couple.

"Can you blame me?" Longwell asked in a low, desperate way. "Wouldn't you get tired of being called a murderer and a killer? Would you like to be known as a Hanging Judge?"

"Nope, I expect I wouldn't, but your friends—"

"Friends!" Longwell echoed scornfully. "I have none! Once, yes—but in the past years they've all disappeared—vanished. Men and women that we considered as friends got to where they would cross the street to avoid us. It has been particularly hard on Mrs. Longwell."

Sam Remington made no comment, seemingly lost in the drone of the onrushing stage, the drumming of the horses as they raced on, each matching the other stride for stride, hoofs striking the baked clay surface of the road in perfect unison.

"Yeh, I reckon I can see how you feel," Sam said at length. "It sure would take a lot of guts—excuse me, ladies—a lot of sand to stay put on a job with things like that going on, no matter how important it was."

"It is important," Longwell said morosely, "and I did it in the best way I could. They call me a hanging judge, but I never sent a man to the gallows who didn't deserve it—and I never hanged an innocent man. I made certain, doubly certain in fact, that I was doing the right thing and what the law dictated I do.

"Yet I've been reviled, cursed, spat upon, threatened, and called the worst of names. My family life has been broken up. My wife, yes my wife, is ashamed of me."

Sophie Longwell half turned, her stolid expression changed, and for the first time she spoke.

"No, John, I never—"

"There's no use trying to keep it from me, Sophie," the jurist said kindly. "I've been aware of it for over a year now. I don't blame you. It's something neither of us has had any control over."

The coach lurched suddenly as a wheel dropped into a chuckhole. Remington slammed up against Stacey Blackburn who, in turn, was thrown against her husband. Sophie Longwell was thrown against the judge, displacing her knitted shawl to a position about her hips.

Sam mumbled under his breath, knowing exactly where they were on the road—at a point where a wash intersected the route to lay a narrow strip of roughness across the route. McElroy, had he been watching and on his toes, could have seen it, slowed the team in time to make the short crossing without subjecting his passengers to a severe jolt.

Dust had thickened inside the coach as pockets of the tan powder trapped in corners and joints of the rocking vehicle exploded to combine with that already spinning about in a choking cloud. Stacey Blackburn coughed discreetly behind a cupped hand and Sophie Longwell brushed at her bloodless lips with a handkerchief. The men straightened themselves on the seat, tugging their clothing into place and resetting their hats as the stage leveled off to resume its fairly even course.

"Doing a job ain't always easy," Sam Remington said,

picking up the conversation where it had been broken off, "but there's them that's got to be done. And it seems to me the good Lord shows a lot of sense in picking the right men to do them.

"Take one like yours—being a judge. You got to have a fellow that ain't afraid of nobody, of nothing. And he's got to have enough sand to do what he knows is right, and the devil with what other folks think about him—"

"You trying to tell me I'm wrong to resign?" Longwell cut in, again gripping the window sill as the stage once again began to sway.

Remington's thick shoulders stirred. "Judge, I ain't trying to tell you nothing—only saying what I think. You're a growed man. You know what's what, specially when it comes down to you, yourself, but I sure hate to think of what'd happen to this country if there wasn't hanging judges around to see that the outlaws didn't take over."

Longwell's jaw tightened slightly and a faint flush mounted in his face. "I agree, but I feel I've done my share and that I've taken all the abuse that should be expected of me. Let someone else shoulder the responsibility. I feel I'm entitled now to live what's left of my life in a normal way—like other men."

The coach had increased speed and the rocking and careening was more pronounced. Remington glanced through the window. They were on a long flat stretch of road that shortly would reach the foot of another grade. What the hell was McElroy pushing the horses so hard for? There was no need. The team could take the slope ahead without even breaking stride.

"Yeh, reckon you are," Remington said. Longwell seemed to be seeking approval of his decision. "Only thing I can say—"

Sam Remington broke off suddenly as the quick, dry rattle of gunshots reached him.

8

Travis Blackburn had come upright on his seat. "Wasn't that shooting?"

Remington nodded tautly. Longwell's features were stiff with disbelief.

"You mean we're being held up? I thought this coach never—"

"I don't know what it means," Sam Remington snapped, continuing to stare out of the window as he sought to locate the source of the gunshots.

The stage, on near level ground prior to reaching the next grade, was steadily gathering momentum and Billy McElroy's voice was now a howl reaching above the sounds of the thundering horses and rattling coach. Another spate of gunfire came, this time louder—nearer. The coach seemed to move even faster.

"Damned fool—he's going to turn us over," Sam muttered, still searching for a glimpse of the gunmen.

The knuckles of J. D. Longwell's fingers showed white where his hand clutched at the window sill. "Why, in heaven's name, would anybody want to hold us up?" he asked in a ragged voice.

Remington, bracing himself, shook his head. "I can't figure it out. We ain't been stopped during all the time I done the driving—and that means better'n ten year. No reason to. Never carry nothing but passengers—and dang few of them lately—and folks traveling usually don't have much cash on them. Unless" —Sam paused, glancing at Blackburn and Longwell— "unless you gents have got full pocketbooks."

"I—we don't have but enough to pay fare," Travis Blackburn said, also holding tight to the edge of the window at his shoulder as he fought to maintain balance in the now wildly swaying vehicle.

The judge said: "We're only carrying a few dollars. I had the bank issue a draft for what little we'd saved."

"There—there must be some other reason," Stacey Blackburn said. She had pressed herself tight against the seat, her features hard lined by fear.

"I can't think of none," Remington murmured. "I only—"

His voice stopped as the stage veered drunkenly, rose onto two wheels, hung briefly, and then whipped sharply back into line as the horses rushed on.

The shooting had become more distinct. Remington, head out of the window, caught sight of the attackers—two riders racing in from that side of the road, firing as they came. Evidently there were others on the opposite flank.

Sam flinched as a bullet drove low into the side of the stage, leaving a dimpled mark where it hit. The first shots had been warnings. The outlaws were now making it clear they meant business. Leaning farther out Remington put his attention on McElroy.

"Pull down—stop!" he shouted above the creaking and groaning of the coach, whipping back and forth. "You're going to put us in the ditch!"

McElroy, using his whip liberally, cursing the horses, half turned.

"Hell with that! I ain't giving in to no goddammed road agents!"

The stage lurched again, once more going crossways and up onto two wheels. The abrupt, violent pivot threw Remington away from the window, sent him hard into the Blackburns. Somewhat dazed, the old driver righted himself, and grasping the window sill, hauled himself back into place.

He could hear Mrs. Longwell weeping. Stacey had wedged herself tight against her husband's side and was covering her face with both hands as if she hoped to shut out the disaster that was overtaking them.

"Do—do something, can't you?" Longwell shouted above the crackling and popping of the coach. The cloud of dust that now filled the vehicle's interior was so thick it all but hid the passengers one from another.

Remington again thrust his head through the window. "McElroy!" he yelled. Bullets were thumping into the sides of the stage with regularity. "McElroy!"

Billy, legs spread, feet braced against the dashboard, again only half turned. The team, heads low, necks outstretched, tails streaming, was pounding along the road at top speed.

"What?"

McElroy's single word answer was a high note on the rushing wind. Sam cupped a hand to his mouth so as to be better heard.

"Pull up—dammit! You're going to kill us all!"

"I ain't about to!" Billy shouted. "I aim to outrun them!"

"Outrun what?" Remington answered angrily, steadying himself in the open window of the reeling stage with his shoulders. "Ain't a horse ever lived that could outrun a bullet!"

"Don't fret!" the young driver replied. "I'll get you through."

Sam drew back. The two outlaws he'd seen moving in on the right were now just ahead and riding parallel to the horses. Leaning across the Blackburns, he looked out the opposite opening. Two men there also. They were keeping pace with the stagecoach as were the others.

"Can't you make him pull up?" Travis Blackburn said as Remington, struggling against the erratic motion of the stage, returned to his seat. "This ain't nothing but pure foolishness."

"For sure," Sam agreed. "All them outlaws've got to do is shoot one of the horses and we'll end up in a heap—and that's just what they'll do if he don't stop."

"Too bad this company doesn't have a guard up there to help him—a man with a shotgun or a rifle," the judge said, mopping at the sweat on his forehead. "Most stagecoaches do."

"Never been any need—"

"There's always a first time. They should've expected it to happen someday."

Remington was turning again to the window. Hindsight was cheap—and not worth considering. . . . The two outlaws were now close—so close that he could make out their features as they turned to snap bullets at the coach. One was light-haired, had a narrow face. The second was a dark, wiry-looking man who took pains when he triggered his weapon, seemingly aiming each time at a specific target.

Sam wished now he'd strapped on his pistol instead of packing it away in his suitcase; he could be making damn good use of it. Again, aware that he was taking a long chance in exposing himself, Remington pushed himself through the window.

"McElroy—pull up! You hear me? Pull up!"

Billy appeared not to hear, continued to remain half crouched, whip laboring as he drove his team on recklessly at top speed.

Sam sank back. He could think of nothing to do. Either the coach would end up a pile of shattered wood in the ditch or the outlaws would bring down one of the horses. In either event the wild ride would come to a halt. He could only hope none of the passengers—at the mercy of Billy McElroy's poor judgment—would be seriously injured or killed, whichever brought it about. He turned a drawn, bleak face to his fellow travelers.

"Ain't nothing we can do," he said through the swirling haze. "Best you get a good hold on something—the edge of your seat maybe, or the window sills—just anything you can steady yourself with. When we turn over you want to try and keep yourself from being thrown out."

"It might be better if you two women would get down on the floor," Longwell suggested. "We can put our legs across you, hold you, perhaps prevent your—"

The coach pitched, rocked, slammed back and forth in a sudden change of motion. Stacey Blackburn screamed, clutched her husband's arm. As abruptly the stage whipped into line, rushed on.

"That was almost it—" Longwell said tensely.

Sam nodded grimly. It would have taken very little more to put the big coach into the ditch. "Close," he murmured.

The shooting appeared to have slacked off. In the next moment he felt the stagecoach begin to slow. A shadow whipped past the window. Sam Remington jerked back as

Stacey Blackburn's scream again filled the vehicle. The fleeting shadow had been Billy McElroy's body hurtling down from the driver's seat, to bounce and roll and become lost in the tangle of brush off the shoulder of the road.

9

"My God—that was him—the driver!" Longwell said in a shocked voice. "The team's running away!"

"They'll shoot the horses for sure now; they'll wreck us," Blackburn said, arm tightening about his wife.

Sam Remington, unhesitating, crowded up close to the door. The stage was rocking and whipping about wildly and he fought to keep from being thrown forcibly to the floor. Reaching for the door handle, he turned it. The hinged panel flew open as the coach wheeled from it, swung back as wind pressure and momentum reversed its motion.

"What—" Blackburn began.

Remington shook his head. There was no time for explanations—and there was only one thing to do; he had to get up on the box, gather in the lines, and bring the panicked team under control. So far the outlaws had not resorted to shooting one of the horses; instead they were closing in on them as if planning to seize the leader's bridles, and in that way halt the stage. Just why they would choose that most dangerous manner he could only wonder.

Pulling his hat down tight on his head, Sam stood up in the doorway of the plunging coach. Extending his arm, he caught one of the baggage rack bars in his hand and again steadied himself against the whipping motion of the stage. It was going to take strength to do what he had in mind and he wasn't certain that he had it in him—but he had to try. The passengers, the horses, the coach as well as he were lost if he didn't do something to halt the runaway—and do it quick.

Placing one foot on the sill of the window next to which he had been sitting, he swung out over the spinning wheel. For a brief moment he was a human pendulum against the curving side of the stagecoach while his free hand groped for purchase also on the baggage rack. And then, as his fingers felt the cold, round iron, he locked them onto it.

Sucking for breath, fighting the motion of the coach, the wind that was tearing at him, and muscles aching, he heaved, bringing his other leg about and placing his right foot alongside the left on the window sill. He hung there for only moments and then pulled himself to the rear of the coach. Still straining for breath but unwilling to waste even a moment, Remington worked his way around the corner of the reeling vehicle onto the slanting canvas boot.

There, hands gripping the rack, toes digging into the slack cover, he was forced to pause. His arms seemed to be weighted with lead, the muscles of his legs were in knots and breathing was difficult—near impossible, but he knew he couldn't quit at that point—not when he was so near.

He rode out a long half minute while he gathered himself, and then putting everything he had into it, he drew himself up onto the roof of the racing stagecoach.

Flat on his belly, spread-eagled, hands fast to the bars of the rack, feet braced against them, Sam rested again.

The outlaws were riding alongside the team, keeping pace, but they had seen him and had ceased their efforts to stop the madly running horses by crowding in on them, apparently electing to hold off and see if he was successful.

Breath restored to near normal, and ignoring his complaining muscles, Remington began to crawl slowly forward. It would have been suicide to rise—even to his knees. The whipping back and forth, the jarring and jolting motion of the stage would have thrown him clear instantly.

He reached the front of the baggage rack, and clinging tight to the end crossbar, crawled over its edge onto the seat. There, taking care, he planted his feet wide apart on the floor board, and grasping the seat rail, released his hold on the baggage rack.

Face taut, strain showing in his eyes, Sam Remington caught up the sagging reins. Those of the off horses had dropped but caught on the round metal step near the brake; those of the near had fallen clear of the dashboard and were trailing in the churning dust in the wake of the wheel horses' heels.

Sam could see no way he could retrieve those as staying on the seat was requiring all his attention at that moment; leaving it, leaning down and trying to reach the loose leathers was out of the question. He would have to try and stop the runaways with half a set of lines, the brake—and his voice.

Snatching up the reins of the off horses, he put a foot on the brake pedal and began to apply a gentle pressure, all the while pulling back on the lines while he shouted to the team. His hope was that Brownie, the near leader, would feel his opposite in harness, slacking off and slow his own pace accordingly. Behind him Dave and Curly would then naturally break their headlong run.

The team began to respond and the sickening sway and lurch of the stage gradually died. But the near horses, free of the reins upon which they relied for guidance and instruction, were not pulling down as Sam hoped, and shortly he had the off horses laying back while the near team fought to continue.

"Whoa—Brownie! Whoa—Dave!" Remington shouted, making himself heard above the screeching of the brake shoes hard against the iron tires of the wheels. "Curly! Whoa! Whoa!"

The pull of the off horses, the drag of the brake, or the familiar sound of his voice—Remington didn't know which, and spent no time in speculation—finally got through to the near team. The lean bay in the lead began to hold back. Immediately the horses behind him broke stride, slowed, and within another fifty yards all had come to a trembling halt.

With sounds of relief coming to him from inside the coach, and aware of the outlaws wheeling in alongside, Remington coolly lowered himself down the front of the stage to where he could reach the loose reins. Then, both sets firmly in hand, he resumed his place on the box.

Dust was swirling around the stage and the foam-flecked horses, as Remington, weary, soaked with sweat from head to toe, turned his attention onto the outlaws now halting, two to each side. He felt a start as one rode in close and looked up at him. It was the young cowhand he'd seen hanging around the depot in Apache Springs just before pulling out.

"You done good, old man," the outlaw said. "Just set tight and don't get no fool notions."

"About doing what?" Remington snapped. "I ain't armed."

"I'm sure glad to hear that. What about your passengers?"

"They ain't carrying weapons either. What the hell do you want? Ain't no money on this stage—'cepting maybe a few dollars. Nothing worth killing a man for."

The outlaw frowned, then added, "Oh, you're talking about that fool driver. That was a dumb stunt he tried. He ought've knowed better."

"Maybe he should've," Sam replied testily, "but you ain't answered my question. What're you wanting?"

"Reckon you could say it's personal, grandpa," the outlaw said, and swinging off his horse strode up to the coach and glanced inside. He nodded in satisfaction, pivoted on a heel, and returning to his mount, went back onto the saddle.

"He's fine," he called to the remaining three men now strung out in a line along the off horses. "I was afeard maybe a stray bullet might've got him, but he's same as new."

"Who're you talking about?" Remington demanded angrily. It had to be either Longwell or Blackburn.

"Don't get your dander up, old man," the outlaw said coldly. "Just you do what you're told and things'll work out fine. Savvy?"

Sam made no reply. He stared at the man's dark, whisker-covered face. Like as not it was Judge Longwell they were after, having in mind to settle an old score of some sort. He reckoned he could only string along with them—for the time being.

"You're dealing the cards," he said at length. "What do you want me to do?"

"There's a grove of cottonwoods on down the road a piece—maybe a mile—"

"I know where it is."

"Want you to drive there and pull off. I'll show you where to stop."

Remington laced the lines, prepared to take his foot off the brake.

"There ain't no big rush—so just take your time," the outlaw said. "Me and my friends'll be riding right along with you so if you go trying something cute, you'll come bouncing down off that seat same as that other driver."

The man spurred forward, riding in close to the coach. Leaning over he put his glance again on the passengers.

"You folks set right where you are—nice and quiet. Any of you tries jumping out and making a run for it'll find hisself full of holes. Goes for you ladies, too."

A muffled answer came from the interior of the stage followed by a question of some sort—inaudible to Sam Remington. The outlaw nodded.

"You'll find out in time, lady," he said, and wheeling his horse, he dropped back to where the others waited.

"Everything's going fine, boys," he said, grinning at his friends, and then lifted his eyes to Remington. "All right, let's go—and you sure better mind your p's and q's."

Mouth set, Sam released the brake, and snapping the lines, shouted to the team. The horses threw themselves into their collars and the stage rolled forward. He guessed he'd find out pretty quick what the holdup was all about.

10

The grove lay a short distance off the road. With two of the outlaws leading and two trailing behind, Sam Remington drove the stagecoach into the first of the thick-trunked, broadly spreading cottonwoods and drew to a halt. The outlaws were off their horses immediately and quickly took up places alongside the coach.

"Come on out of there, everybody!"

At the command of the one Sam had noticed at the stage depot and who appeared to be the leader, the door opened and Stacey Blackburn, face pale, eyes mirroring her fear and somewhat disheveled, stepped down onto the short grass. A low whistle came from two of the men.

Sophie Longwell followed, stiff and prim, her shawl clutched about her shoulders. The judge came next and finally, Travis Blackwell, his features set and angry.

"Means you, too, grandpa," one of the outlaws said, and beckoned to Remington.

The old driver secured the lines, wrapping them about the handrail of the seat. Climbing down, he took a place in the line formed by the others.

"Search them—"

Remington shook his head. "I already told you ain't none of us armed."

"Reckon you did but I ain't of a notion to be taking your word for it," the outlaw leader said coolly. "I aim to make sure."

Two of his followers stepped up, one grinning broadly. He made a hasty examination of Blackburn's person and turned to Stacey.

"This sure is going to be a pleasure," he said.

Travis Blackburn moved in front of his wife. His eyes sparked and a flush had mounted in his drawn face.

"You lay a hand on her and I'll—"

The outlaw, a dark, young man with a clipped mustache, paused. Hooking thumbs in his belt he settled back on his heels, cocked his head to one side and considered Blackburn. Nearby his partner had finished his probing of John and Sophie Longwell, and with the other two outlaws, was watching intently.

"You'll do what, sodbuster?"

Travis Blackburn did not hesitate. "I'll kill you."

"Do tell! Just how you aim to do that?"

"I'll find a way. Nobody touches my wife."

"Maybe you'd like to have a go at me right now," the outlaw said.

Blackburn took a half a step forward. At once the young leader of the quartet moved up and laid a hand on his friend.

"Back off, Hank," he said. "There ain't no time for that."

Hank shrugged him aside. "Far as I can tell we ain't got nothing but time seeing as how we got to wait around for your brother."

"You heard me—cut it out! If you got some idea about that woman save it till later. Right now I want you and Dogie to take the horses down to the creek and picket them. They ain't been watered all day."

Hank, arms folded across his chest, studied the outlaw leader in the same amused manner that he had shown Travis Blackburn.

"And what'll you be doing, Mister Vaughn?"

"Talking—"

Hank did not move. Dogie, a tall, blond, stepped up, laid a hand on his shoulder. "Come on. Willie knows what he's doing."

"Maybe," Hank said, relenting. And then as he turned away, added, "I'm getting goddammed tired of him ordering me around—I can tell you that."

Dogie . . . Hank . . . Willie Vaughn . . . Sam Remington rolled the names about in his mind. None struck a familiar chord. Still simmering, he put his attention on the latter.

"You going to tell us what this is all about or ain't you?"

Vaughn, a hand resting on the butt of his holstered pistol, shook his head warningly. "Best you keep out of this, old man. It ain't none of your butt-in."

"They're passengers on my stage. That sure'n hell makes it my business!" Remington replied hotly.

"Not no more," Willie Vaughn replied evenly. "Just you back off, too, and keep your trap shut." He motioned to the fourth outlaw, a wiry, older man. "Charlie, keep an eye on the old fool—he's sort of feisty. If he gets cute lay your iron up against the side of his head."

Charlie grinned, moved nearer to Remington. Willie, swung back to the passengers, centered his attention on John Longwell.

"How's the hanging business, Judge?"

Longwell frowned. "I'm not sure I know what you're talking about."

"The hell you don't—hanging's your meat! The name Vaughn mean anything to you?"

The jurist repeated the name, his forehead knotted into a frown. Then, "No, I can't say that it does."

"How about Lonnie Vaughn?"

Again Longwell gave it thought. Dogie and Hank were disappearing into the brush leading their four horses behind them, pointing for the small creek that cut a narrow path through the grove. Travis Blackburn, an arm around his wife, was listening in stony silence to what was being said while a step back of the judge Sophie Longwell maintained her icy composure.

"Can't recall a Lonnie Vaughn—"

"By God, you ought to!" Willie exploded angrily. "He was my brother. Was you that lynched him about six months ago—for something he didn't do!"

Longwell stiffened. "If he was sentenced to hang, he was guilty. You can be certain of that."

Sam Remington was staring at the jurist. That John Longwell failed to recall the name of a man he had sentenced to die was hard to believe, but it appeared to be the fact. Was it possible all the things that had been said about the judge were true? Could he be a heartless, cruel man who took delight in handing out the death penalty?

"You standing there flat-footed saying you don't remember Lonnie?" Willie Vaughn pressed in a tight voice.

"I simply administer the law," the judge said, utterly cool. "Criminals—outlaws brought before me are only that. They're never individuals. Names mean absolutely nothing. I am interested only in guilt or innocence and rule accordingly."

Vaughn studied Longwell in the hush that followed. Finally he shrugged. "Well, you're going to be in on the other end of some ruling this time, mister. My brother

Jake's on his way now—and he's bringing a jury along with him."

Longwell brushed nervously at his lips. "I—I don't understand—"

"You will. We're aiming to hold us a court right here in this grove where there's aplenty of trees. We're going to hold court, try you, same as you did Lonnie, and after the jury finds you guilty we're going to string you up—just like you had Lonnie done."

Sophie Longwell's reserve broke. A hand flew to her mouth as a cry escaped her throat.

"No!"

Willie Vaughn transferred his bleak attention to her. "Yes'm, that's how it's to be. Jake and me've been hoping and waiting for our chance. You all made it easy when you decided to pull up stakes and move."

Travis Blackburn cleared his throat. He spat. "You can't get away with that. It ain't nothing but murder."

"So was Lonnie getting hung," Willie said quietly. "And we'll get away with it, all right. It'll be all over and done with before anybody knows what happened because there ain't nobody looking for the stage—ain't that so, old man?"

Vaughn had swung his glance to Remington. Sam shrugged noncommittally. "Folks in the station at Apache Springs—"

"Don't try horsing me! They know you pulled out. Them at Springerville don't know you're coming. Neither does Halverson. Me and Jake got the lay of the land before we made our move. We figured it all out."

Dogie and Hank, their chore completed, were coming back into the half circle, the roving, hungry eyes of the latter raking Stacey boldly.

"What about us?" Blackburn said. "There's no need

keeping us around. We ain't never done anything to you or your brother."

"You mean I ought to let you climb aboard the stage and head out?" Willie said with a sly smile.

"There's no reason to hold us—"

"The hell there ain't. First thing you'd do would be to light out for help. I ain't no fool. You're all going to stay put. After the trial's over Jake'll decide what he wants to do with you."

Longwell, face grim, raised his eyes to the outlaw. "Blackburn's right. There's no need to punish the others. It's me that you want to settle with. Let them go and I'll give you my word I'll give you no problem."

Willie Vaughn laughed. "You ain't going to give me no trouble, Judge. There's four of us here to see to that. Now, I want you all back in that stage and setting quiet. My brother and the others'll be coming in a couple of hours—all the way from Springerville just to be on hand for the doings. Meantime, me and the boys'll be setting and watching and keeping an eye on you. Any of you steps outside—gets shot."

"All 'cepting the gal," Hank said. "I've took quite a fancy to her and I sure don't want no bullet holes messing up her pretty hide."

Travis Blackburn's features again darkened and his hands shaped themselves into rock-hard fists. For a long breath he glared at the outlaw and then taking his wife by the arm, guided her to the coach and all but pushed her into it. He wheeled then, attention again on Hank. Remington thought for a moment that he intended to take on the outlaw, weapon or not, but if such had been in his mind he reconsidered and climbed into the stage and seated himself beside Stacey.

Hank laughed and scrubbed at his chin. Willie Vaughn

gave him a hard look and motioned to the remaining passengers.

"Rest of you—inside. And be damn sure you stay there."

Longwell, with Sophie preceding, crossed to the coach and entered. Sam Remington jerked a thumb at the team.

"Them horses need watering, too. McElroy run them mighty hard."

"They ain't hurting," Willie said curtly, and drawing his pistol, waggled it pointedly. "Climb aboard, old man."

Remington walked slowly to the coach and drew himself inside. Hank had not moved and was still standing legs spraddled, arms folded, eyes on Stacey, little more than a shadow in the dark interior of the vehicle.

"Just forget what you're thinking, Hank," Vaughn said coolly, pistol still in his hand. "After Jake gets here you can do whatever you goddammed please. Right now I ain't taking no chances on you or anybody else fouling things up."

Hank pivoted in a deliberate, coiled sort of way. "I been wondering something, Willie."

"Yeh—what?" Vaughn's tone was cautious.

"If you're big enough to back up all them orders you been handing out."

A stillness settled over Vaughn. "I reckon there's only one way you'll ever know," he said softly.

"Yeh, expect that's the truth—"

"Willie's right, Hank," Dogie said quickly, breaking the tension and once again breaching a danger-filled moment. "I sure would hate to face Jake if we was the cause of something going wrong."

Hank did not remove his sullen stare from Vaughn. "How's me having myself a time with that gal going to make something go wrong?"

"That big yahoo of a husband of hers ain't going to let you get close to her without a fight. That'll lead to shooting and that there judge maybe'll get hit, then there'll be hell to pay. Anyways, you can wait a couple hours or so. She'll be just as good then as now, maybe even better."

The man called Charlie bobbed in agreement, and taking Willie Vaughn by the shoulder, pushed him about gently and started him off toward a nearby spur of trees that jutted out from the main grove.

"That's for true, Hank. Things always seem to get better when a man has to wait for them."

Hank's rigid frame eased. His partly raised arms settled against his sides, and throwing a final glance at the stagecoach, he shambled off for the spur.

11

Pressed against her husband's chest, Stacey Blackburn wept raggedly. Travis, his broad face frozen, patted her quietly as he endeavored to comfort and reassure her.

Longwell, palms of his hands pressed together, fingers interlaced, elbows on his knees as he leaned forward, shook his head. "What are we going to do?" he asked in a strained voice.

"What the hell can we do?" Blackburn demanded in a savage tone.

Stacey raised her torn, tear-stained face and looked at Remington. "They intend to kill us all, don't they—just like they did that poor driver?"

Sam forced a smile. "Maybe not—"

"You know they do!" the girl cried and began to sob brokenly. "That's why I hate this country so—why I won't live here in this—this wilderness! There's nothing but violence—death and cruelty. It's not a fit place—not even for animals!"

Stacey's voice faded, the words of frustration ended. She pulled away from Travis, and face buried in her hands, began to weep anew. Abruptly Sophie Longwell came from her shell of cold reserve. She nodded crisply to Blackwell.

"You will exchange seats with me."

There was no give in her tone, only the inflexibility of iron. Travis Blackburn moved forward immediately, allowed the older woman to take his place while he settled beside the judge. Gathering the girl in her arms, Sophie held her close, as a mother would a small child, murmuring softly all the while.

"Everything will be all right, dear. Don't you worry."

Longwell's distraught eyes searched those of Sam Remington. "Not much hope for us, is there?"

"John!" Sophie scolded.

The jurist shrugged. "It's best we face up to the truth. There's nothing to be gained by fooling ourselves. I'm only sorry to be the cause of it."

"Being sorry doesn't help much," Sophie said acidly. "I always knew something like this would happen one day—that the kin of some of those men would try to get revenge."

"I only did what was expected of me—"

"Perhaps, but you didn't have to become a judge. You could have kept on with your law practice. I told you then that it was a mistake to accept the appointment but you wouldn't listen."

Longwell, patient, heard the woman out, his attention still on Remington. When she was finished, he said: "You got any ideas?"

Sam brushed at his mustache. The outlaw called Dogie had gotten to his feet and was walking off toward the deep brush where the horses were picketed.

"I'm trying to figure up something, but I'm not having much luck. One thing, Willie and Hank are about to crawl each other's frame. Seems to be bad blood between them. If they get to mixing it up we maybe'll get the chance to do something."

"You don't think they'll let the rest of us go when this Jake gets here? It's the judge they're wanting," Blackburn said, his voice lowering at the last as if he didn't wish the jurist to hear.

Remington stirred. "What they're planning is murder—and they sure won't want to leave anybody alive to tell about it."

The reply brought a fresh surge of weeping from Stacey Blackburn. Sophie, glaring at Sam, redoubled her efforts to quiet the girl.

"Sure wish I'd brought my gun," Travis muttered, swiping at the sweat on his forehead with the back of a hand. "Knew I should've worn it."

"Got mine in my suitcase—in the boot," Remington said. "I'm wishing the same thing."

"There's no chance of you getting it," Longwell said. "Minute you'd step outside they'd shoot you down."

Over in the open grassland beyond the trees a meadow lark whistled cheerfully. Remington stared thoughtfully off into that direction, searching his mind all the while for an idea—a scheme of any sort—that would enable him and his passengers to escape. What the judge had said about his getting his pistol was true; the outlaws, squatting in the shade no more than twenty yards away, would stop him before he could reach the end of the coach. But he had to come up with a plan of some sort.

Despite the fact he'd not been the driver, and therefore not in command of the stage as it pulled out of Apache Springs—was actually not even an employee of the company—Sam Remington, nevertheless, felt an obligation to the passengers in this hour of crisis; when a man has carried the burden of responsibility for those in his charge for the major part of his life, he does not discard it simply because he no longer is being paid in dollars and cents for doing so.

And if anything was to be done, he would be the one who would have to do it, Sam was sure of that. He could expect little from Longwell, and less from Travis Blackburn, young, new to the country, impulsive, and with no experience in dealing with men of the caliber they were up against, who would likely only get them into deeper trouble, if such was possible. The women, of course, were out of it altogether.

"We've got a little time," he said, eyes moving to Dogie now returning from his visit to the horses. The outlaw was carrying a near full bottle of whiskey which apparently had been stowed in his saddlebags. "Something could turn up."

"Just what?" Blackburn said wearily. "There won't be anybody looking for the stage—and they couldn't see us back here behind the trees if there was."

"I know that, but we best keep hoping," Remington replied, and changing the subject for the sake of the girl, voiced a question that had earlier lodged in his mind.

"Judge, that true what you said about not even knowing the names of the men that've come before you for sentencing—or was you just saying that to Willie Vaughn?"

"It's true, I suppose," Longwell answered. "My only interest in the matter was in seeing that the law was upheld. Why should a man's name make any difference?"

"I don't know. It just seems it should."

"I can't agree with you," Longwell said. "Justice is blind, and should be, if it's to consider cases fairly and impartially. I think it's better if a judge doesn't know who he is judging. There's no favoritism then. But why are we talking about my—"

"Guess you're right when you look at it that way,"

Remington said, his attention again on Willie Vaughn and the others. They were passing the bottle around, and the man called Charlie was on his feet stretching and yawning as if in need of sleep. That they all would doze off could be wishful thinking but it was a possibility.

"My husband is an honest man," Sophie Longwell said suddenly, as if coming to the defense of the jurist. "Don't ever question that."

"I'm not," Remington said, "and I didn't aim for it to sound like I was. I only wanted to get something cleared up in my head."

Charlie had settled down again. Shoulders to a tree trunk, legs extended before him, he appeared to be on the verge of napping. But the remaining outlaws showed no indication of following his example. Hank was nursing the bottle of liquor, Dogie was rolling a cigarette, and Vaughn seemed lost in the distant whistling of the meadow lark.

They were a hard-looking bunch, Sam thought. Their clothing was worn, faded, their boots scuffed and run down at the heels, their hats ragged and with uneven brims. Dogie, he'd noted earlier, had but one spur. All were well armed, however, and had the grim-set manner of men accustomed to using their weapons.

"How long do you figure it'll be until the other brother—Jake, I think they called him—will get here?"

To Longwell's question Sam said: "Your guess is good as mine, Judge. Couple of hours, according to Willie. Don't think he knows exactly. Appears they had this all worked out ahead of time. Willie and that bunch with him waited along the road for us after being sure the judge would be aboard."

"How'd he know that for sure?" Blackburn asked.

"Seen him hanging around the stage depot before we pulled out. Soon as we'd climbed into the stage, he rode off."

Longwell frowned. "Didn't that start you to wondering about him?"

"Why should it? Looked like some everyday cowhand to me. Anyways, there's always folks standing around a depot watching a coach come in or leave."

"I can't figure why this brother Jake wasn't here waiting—"

"Me neither. Could be they were all in Springerville, then when word got to them from some friend up the line that you and your missus was going to be on the coach today, Jake sent Willie on ahead to set things up."

"Jake probably had something to tend to," Travis Blackburn added, again brushing at the sweat on his face. "I sure wish there was something we could do. Hate just setting here waiting—like cattle in a slaughter chute."

The ill-chosen comment brought a renewal of Stacey Blackburn's sobs but her husband seemed not to notice. Longwell continued to rub his palms together nervously, and one of the horses in the team stamped and blew noisily, starting a jingling of harness metal. They were tired after the hard, fast run Billy McElroy had put them through, and Sam wished he'd been able to unhitch them and take them down to the creek for water, but Willie Vaughn had refused his request.

Just as well. Let them stand in harness. If an opportunity for escape presented itself it would require the use of the team and stagecoach and they would need to be ready.

Dogie had joined Charlie in a reclining position, head dropped forward, hat over his eyes. Hank was staring off in the direction of the coach and Willie Vaughn, pistol in his hands, was idly twirling the cylinder.

"I've been thinking about what Blackburn said a while back," Longwell began, stirring on his seat. "It's me they want, all right. What if I jumped out of here and rushed them? You think you'd have time enough to get away?"

Remington shook his head. "They'd cut you down before you got ten feet—"

"Maybe not. The way I see it, they want me alive for this trial they're planning to hold—and for the execution. If I could create enough confusion you might have time enough to get up there on the seat and drive off."

"You'd be wasting yourself, Judge. They'd shoot me before I could pick up the lines. They've got no reason to keep me living."

"That's a foolish thought, John," Sophie Longwell said, her tone somewhat kinder. "Brave—but foolish. It would serve no purpose."

Stacey Blackburn sat up. Her face was drawn and her eyes were filled with resignation as if she had reconciled herself to the fate that lay ahead for all of them. Travis studied her briefly and then turned to the window.

"Looks like a couple of them are sleeping. Maybe, if the other two—"

"I've been watching for that," Sam said. "If they'll all drop off, I'll slip out the other door, circle around, and get my gun."

"There's another'n stretching out," Blackburn said in a tense voice. "That leaves only Vaughn. Now, if he'll just do like the others—"

Silent, taut, they watched the outlaws. Willie Vaughn continued to finger his weapon—hefting it, spinning the cylinder, sighting down its barrel—as the minutes crept slowly by. Abruptly Dogie drew himself to a sitting position and reached into a pocket for his cigarette makings.

A long sigh escaped Travis Blackburn's lips as he and the others in the coach settled back in disappointment.

"I guess we can forget about that," he said in a falling voice.

12

The minutes dragged on. It grew warm inside the coach. Sophie Longwell removed her shawl, folded it neatly and laid it across her knees. The judge loosened his necktie and Stacey Blackburn discarded her jacket. Insects clacked loudly in the grass and weeds nearby while the meadow larks out on the flat continued their whistling.

"How long have we been here?" the girl asked. Her features had taken on a slack, lifeless cast. It was evident she had given up all hope.

"Hour—at least," Longwell replied.

"I expect they will be coming soon," Stacey said, and reaching across, she laid her hand on that of her husband. "I'm sorry, Travis. I guess I haven't been much of a wife to you."

Blackburn shifted uncomfortably. "You did the best you could with what little we had. I—"

Sam Remington raised a quick hand for silence. The faint rap of hoofs was hanging in the still air. Alarm sprang into Stacey's eyes. Sophie Longwell lowered her head as if to pray while her husband stiffened slowly. Blackburn, frowning, stared at Remington as he listened.

"Only a couple of horses," he said as the drumming grew louder. "Figured there'd be more."

Sam nodded. "It's not Jake and them. These riders are coming from Apache Springs way."

Everyone stirred, hope brightening in their eyes. Stacey said, "You mean it's not the other outlaws?"

"They'll be coming in from the south—Springerville, so Willie said."

"Do—do you think they're looking for us?"

"Doubt it. Likely a couple of cowhands on their way to somewhere. Good chance they'll swing in here to water their horses. Riders do a lot of the time."

Blackburn pointed to the outlaws. All were on their feet and looking in the direction of the road, not visible to them because of the trees.

"They've heard them coming, too—and they'll be waiting for them."

Remington made no comment as the rhythmic beat of the horses drew nearer. If the riders did turn off the road and enter the grove they would not see the stagecoach or Vaughn and his crowd until they were upon them—and then it would be too late to act. They should be warned.

Sam turned his attention to the side of the coach away from the outlaws. If he could manage to slip out the door, make a dash for the nearest trees, and get within their shelter before being seen, he would be in a position to head off the riders and enlist their aid.

The trick would be to gain the thick stand of cottonwoods, some forty or fifty feet distant. With a bit of luck he could do it—and it was sure as hell worth a try.

He paused as a second thought came to him. Even if he failed the gunshots would draw the notice of the riders, bring them in to investigate. Such would, at least, provide a slim chance of rescue for the passengers.

The sound of the running horses was loud and firm as Remington pulled himself forward on the seat and prepared to move to the opposite side of the coach and make his try. He bucked his head at Longwell and the others.

"I aim to try and head those riders off and warn them. You folks just set tight."

Longwell caught at the old driver's arm. "Those outlaws will see you—shoot—"

"Maybe," Remington agreed laconically, reaching through the window for the door handle. "If I don't make it, good luck."

He twisted the curved bit of metal, allowed the hinged panel to swing back, holding tightly to it and permitting it to do so slowly so as to prevent any undue noise. With it open, he edged forward—hesitated. The hoof beats had come to a peak and seemed to be receding.

"They ain't stopping," Travis Blackburn said in a desperate, disappointed way. "They're going straight on."

Once more piled-up tension within the coach broke and melted away. Stacey settled back, brushing at her eyes. Judge Longwell shrugged and turned to look at the outlaws. They had relaxed their sharp surveillance of the open area at the end of the grove where the riders would have first appeared; the possibility of intrusion past, they were again seeking their ease.

Remington, leaving the door wide in the interest of coolness, returned to his seat. Luck was not with them; he would have laid ten-to-one odds the riders would stop, rest, and water their horses. The grove was a natural break in the journey from Apache Springs to Halverson's way station.

"I guess there's no hope now," Stacey murmured.

Sophie Longwell patted her on the knee. "Don't give up yet. There's always hope—until the very last."

Sam considered the outlaws. His scheme to warn the passing riders and enlist their aid had failed not because of him but due to the contrariness of luck. He must come up with another idea now. Time was growing short.

The men were in a small cluster, probably talking over the near emergency the passing pilgrims on the road had posed. They'd all be fully awake now and he might as well forget about taking them unawares while they napped.

Sam's eyes narrowed. Willie Vaughn, with the one called Charlie, had risen and were strolling leisurely off toward their horses. Hank and Dogie watched them until they had gained the first outcropping of brush, and then both rose and started for the coach.

"Trouble—coming," he warned softly.

At once Travis Blackburn said: "I'll take my seat back, ma'am," trading places with Sophie Longwell.

The two outlaws halted alongside the stage. Hank, tossing aside the empty whiskey bottle he held in his hand, reached out and opened the door. Stepping in close, he grinned at Stacey.

"All right, girlie, time for us to take a little walk."

Stacey recoiled against her husband. Remington pushed forward into the opening. "Leave her alone!"

Hank's thick arm shot out. His fingers wrapped about the driver's wrist. Jerking, he pulled Remington through the doorway, sending him sprawling onto the ground.

"Mind your own knitting, grandpa," he snarled, and pistol now in hand, he moved back into the doorway of the stage. "Come on," he commanded, grasping the girl by the arm. "I ain't fooling around no longer."

"Let her be!" Travis Blackburn yelled and threw himself at the outlaw.

Hank lashed out with his pistol, catching the man across the face with it. As Blackburn rocked to one side, he dragged the struggling, sobbing Stacey into the open.

Remington coming to his feet lunged at the outlaw. Dogie stepped forward quickly, caught Sam with a shoulder, and drove him into the front wheel of the stage. The old driver rebounded as breath exploded from his lungs and went down again. Stacey was crying, protesting, fighting the broadly grinning Hank every step as he sought to lead her into the trees.

"You're sure something of a wildcat!" he said, holstering his weapon in order to make use of both hands. "Come on, Dogie—give some help with this here little—"

In that next moment the long shape of Travis Blackburn came hurtling through the doorway of the coach. He drove into Hank full force, knocking Stacey clear, sending her full length to the ground.

"Goddam you!" Hank grated, dragging at the pistol on his hip.

Blackburn kicked out and knocked the outlaw's hand away from the weapon. He surged in, a man seemingly gone wild; he caught Hank by the shirt front with his left hand and smashed a hard right to the jaw. The outlaw staggered back, cursing in pain.

Remington, on his knees, still sucking deep for breath, drew himself upright. This could be the moment he was looking for; if he and Blackburn, and Longwell, could overcome Hank and Dogie while Vaughn and Charlie were elsewhere, get their guns—then deliverance was at hand.

"Out here, Judge!" he rasped hoarsely at Longwell, crouched in the doorway of the stage, and lunged straight at Dogie.

The blond outlaw spun. As Sam rushed in he struck with his pistol. The blow skittered off the older man's head, landing solidly on his neck. Once more he went down.

Dazed, Remington hung there, vaguely aware that Longwell was out of the stagecoach but standing motionless, that Sophie was helping Stacey back to her seat—and that Blackburn and Hank were standing toe to toe slugging it out. Dogie, weapon leveled, had pulled back a few steps and was covering him.

Hank wilted as Blackburn smashed a solid fist into his jaw. He caught himself, came back up. Again Travis rocked him with merciless blows. The outlaw's legs began to tremble. He wavered uncertainly.

"Back off!" Dogie ordered suddenly, turning his pistol on Blackburn.

Travis, breathing hard, hesitated, then came half around. His face was smeared with blood from nose and crushed lips but a fire blazed fierce and bright in his eyes. Fists at his sides, he took a step toward Dogie, totally ignoring the cocked weapon leveled at him.

The outlaw tensed. "Don't try it—or I'll blow your damned head off!"

The harsh threat jarred Blackburn. He halted, frowning. Raising a hand he swiped at the dust and sweat clouding his eyes.

"Look out!" Remington shouted in sudden alarm.

Hank had lunged to his feet, and crouched low, was charging Travis from behind. Blackburn jerked away. Slamming his hands together, he locked his fingers to form a club, and as the outlaw rushed in, he brought his fist cudgel down upon the man's shoulders with all his strength. Hank fell hard, little powdery clouds exploding from beneath his body as it came in contact with the ground.

"Hold it!"

Willie Vaughn's voice was like the crack of a whip in the sudden hush. Remington pulled himself back to his feet and faced the outlaw through the thin pall hovering about the men. Blackburn lowered his arms, wheeled also to face Vaughn and Charlie, hurrying up.

"What the hell's going on here?" Willie began and then broke off.

Hank, pistol in his hand, was upright. Pivoting swiftly, he swung his heavy weapon in a full arc. It caught Travis Blackburn on the side of the head, dropping him like a sledged steer.

13

Stacey Blackburn's piercing scream echoed along the wall of pine trees. She came out of the stagecoach in a quick leap, rushed to her husband, and fell to her knees at his side.

"Oh, Travis!" she moaned, lifting his head and resting it against her leg. Blood was flowing freely from the gash made by the pistol and he appeared to be lifeless. "They've killed you!"

Sophie Longwell moved up to kneel beside her. Sam Remington crossed to the fallen man also, beckoning to John Longwell as he did.

"Give me some help here, Judge. We've got to put him back inside the stage, out of the sun. We'll be needing that canteen of water up on the driver's seat, too."

Longwell, ignoring the silent, scowling outlaws, hurriedly obtained the tin container, and tossing it into the coach, stepped in to assist Remington. Nearby Willie Vaughn, hands on hips, legs spread, was facing Hank.

"Told you to lay off that gal till Jake got here—"

Hank pulled off his hat and dusted himself indifferently. "I don't see that it matters none."

"I don't give a good goddam what you don't see!"

Vaughn snapped, his voice sharp. "I told you to leave her alone."

Hank replaced his hat and gently probed his jaw where Blackburn had landed a telling blow. "I reckon I'm growed enough to do what I want."

"You sure ain't old enough it seems to do what you're told! You been bucking me and Jake mighty regular lately, and it ain't setting good with either one of us. I aim to tell him about this when he shows up."

"Suit yourself," Hank said lightly, "but me having myself some fun with that gal wouldn't be hurting neither one of you any."

"I ain't saying it would but I told you to forget it but you went right on ahead anyway—"

"Like I said, I'm growed enough to do what I please. I don't need to take orders from you—or Jake."

Dogie and Charlie had turned away, drifting back to the trees where they had been waiting. Willie, his face taut, nodded coldly to Hank.

"I aim to tell Jake you said that; I'll let him straighten you out."

"Sure, sure," Hank muttered as he swaggered off in the wake of the two others.

Willie's angry eyes followed him for a few moments and then, coming around, he crossed to the stage. Remington and the judge had laid the unconscious Blackburn on the seat. Stacey was sitting at one end, his head cushioned on her lap, while Sophie Longwell held a fold of white cloth soaked with water from the canteen to his wound.

Sam halted outside the open door, and with Longwell at his shoulder, he turned to face the outlaw.

"He's hurt bad. Ain't come to yet."

Willie Vaughn shrugged. "Climb back inside, both of you," he directed. "And stay there."

Longwell immediately entered the coach. Remington did not stir. "He'll be needing some more water, I expect. It be all right if I go down to the creek and fill the canteen?"

"Forget it," Vaughn said flatly. "Him coming to or not ain't going to make any difference far as I can see. . . . Get inside."

Sam caught the edge of the window in his hand and drew himself into the coach. The outlaw waited until he had seated himself beside Longwell, and then slamming the door shut, wheeled and stalked off toward his companions.

"Travis is going to die, isn't he?" Stacey said in a low voice. It was more a statement of fact than a question.

Sophie poured more water on the compress she had evidently made from a strip of her petticoat. "He needs a doctor," she said, avoiding a direct reply.

Stacey began to rock back and forth, weeping quietly. "It won't matter. We're all going to die, anyway."

"Don't give up hoping," the older woman countered, repeating earlier words. "Not yet."

"What's there to hope for?" Stacey said in a dragging tone. "There's nothing we—anybody—can do."

Remington, a glimmer of an idea beginning to take shape in his mind, threw his glance to the outlaws. They were squatting on their heels in the shade of the big cottonwoods, smoking and talking back and forth.

"I was just thinking," Sam said, coming back to face the others in the coach, "it could be I can do something."

Longwell swung hurriedly to him. "The position we're in, we don't have anything to lose. What is it?"

"The horses—the ones Vaughn and his bunch are riding—they tied them up along the creek."

"Yes, but what good will they—"

"If I can get down there to them without being spotted and stampede them, it'll maybe give us time to pull out of here when they go chasing after them."

Sophie Longwell paused in her ministering, giving Sam's words intent consideration. The judge nodded.

"It could work all right if they react like I believe they will."

"I expect it'll sort of catch them by surprise, and then during the confusion while they light out after the horses I ought to have time enough to get back here, climb up on the box, and pull out."

The jurist leaned forward, his features intent, and nodded. "The road's not too far—and the trees'll hide us as soon as we round the end of the grove."

"What I was figuring, once we're back on the road, we can make a run for Halverson's. I expect we can get there easy ahead of Vaughn and them. It'll take them some time to catch up their horses."

"What if they see you down there along the creek and start shooting?"

"It'd be too bad for me, that's sure, but I don't think they will. It's pretty brushy, and I'll take care to stay low. The big problem is not letting them see me moving after I'm out of the stage."

Longwell glanced out the window on the back side of the coach. The door was still standing open just as Remington had earlier left it. "It'll be no trouble at first. There's a clearing on below a piece, however."

"That's the part I'm worrying about. I need something to hold their attention while I get across it."

"Maybe I can help," Stacey Blackburn said quietly.

Remington shifted his glance to her. He hadn't thought her to be listening, assuming her to be so wrapped up in worry over Travis that nothing else was getting through to her.

"How?" Longwell asked.

"If your wife would exchange places with me, hold Travis's head, I could step outside and do something that would attract those—those—"

"We don't want them coming up to the coach," Remington warned.

"I understand. I could perhaps lift my dress, take off my petticoat as if we were needing it for bandages—or I could remove my shirtwaist—"

"Either one'll work," Sam said, nodding, "long as you get right back into the stage."

"How much time will you need?"

"A few seconds—half a minute at the most."

Stacey smiled wanly. "I can manage it."

"Good. I'll slip out, move to that first stand of bushes. Then you show yourself—slam the door so's I'll know you've made your move. That'll be the signal for me to head for the creek."

At once Stacey gently lifted Travis's head and slipped off the seat. Sophie Longwell quickly moved into her vacated place.

"I'm ready," the girl said.

Sam grinned at her. She had more spunk than he'd thought. "Remember one thing now—don't lose no time getting back aboard. You stay out there too long you'll have Hank coming for you again—the others, too, maybe."

"I understand."

"Another thing—stay ready to go. I'll climb right up onto the box, cut the team around, and head for the road fast as I can—which'll take only a few seconds. There won't be no time to wait for nothing."

"We'll be ready," Longwell assured him, and then added; "It would be a good thing if you could get your hands on your gun. Wouldn't take but a bit more—"

"We'll have to pass that up," Remington cut in. "The big thing's to get out there on the road and running for Halverson's."

"He's right, John," Mrs. Longwell said. "You go with him."

Sam frowned. "I'm not sure that's a good idea."

"Why isn't it? There's no need for him to stay here—and there are four horses. It will take two of you only half as long to untie and chase them off as it would just one."

Longwell nodded vigorously. "And I should be helping you—sharing the risk. You wouldn't be in this fix if it wasn't for me."

Sam Remington mulled it about in his mind and finally assented. "You'll have to keep low—and move fast," he said as he removed his hat.

Twisting about he hung the headgear on the hook at the rear of the window. Only a portion of the brim was visible but to the outlaws it would appear there was someone sitting back on the seat.

"You ready?" he asked, glancing at the judge when he had completed the precaution.

"Ready," the jurist said, and hunching down, he moved through the door opening into the shadows lying at the side of the stagecoach.

Remington followed closely on his heels. Halting beside Longwell, he looked back at Stacey Blackburn.

"Count to ten—slow, then go ahead," he said.

Stacey's answer was a faint smile.

14

Moving out in front of Longwell, Sam Remington hunched low and crossed quickly to a thick clump of rabbitbush. There, behind the gray-green shrub he halted.

Longwell, easing in beside him and breathing hard, muttered: "I'm not used to this."

Remington nodded. "Years kind of catch up with a man for sure," he agreed.

The solid thud of the stagecoach door being closed reached them through the warm stillness. "That'll be the girl," Sam said, and rising slightly, pointed to a dark stand of brush a hundred yards or so away. "Horses are right about in there."

"Lead the way," the jurist said.

Sam threw a hasty glance toward the outlaws. They were partly visible through the screen of intervening growth. Those that he could see were staring in the direction of the stage. Whatever it was that Stacey Blackburn had chosen to do was drawing their attention—and holding it. Remington hoped that in her anxiety to assist in the escape and thereby enable them to get Travis to a doctor as soon as possible, she would not go too far.

Bent low, Sam spurted from behind the clump of brush. He crossed the first narrow strip of open ground, gaining the shelter of another stand of tangled growth. Longwell, now sucking deep for wind was at his heels.

Remington, little better off himself, spent a few moments resting, and then aware that Stacey should be concluding her act shortly, and that a second band of cleared meadow was yet ahead, again bolted into the open and legged it for the fringe of heavy shrubbery that stood along the creek.

Reaching there he turned and bucked his head at Longwell. "Reckon we made it," he said, laboring to get the words out.

Back up where the stagecoach waited, the sound of the door slamming shut came again. John Longwell wiped away the sweat on his forehead and grinned tautly. "Just in time, too, it seems. . . . We close to the horses?"

Sam pointed at the winding line of willows that twisted in and out among the trees. "That's the creek. You can't see the horses but I figure they're somewhere around that big cottonwood—the one with the log laying next to it."

He didn't wait for any comment from Longwell, but struck out immediately at a trot, keeping on the grass to avoid making any sound, taking advantage of the mountain mahogany, scrub oak, and other rank growth that filled the glade. He didn't think it was possible for the outlaws, should they turn their attention toward the creek, to see them but he was taking no chance.

"Got to do this fast," he said gustily over his shoulder as they hurried on. "I don't know how much time we've got before the rest of the outfit rides in, but it sure can't be long."

Longwell, conserving his breath, nodded.

They came to the big cottonwood and halted beside it. Remington had guessed right; four horses were standing off a few yards to their left. Short ropes secured them to a fallen sapling at the edge of the creek.

"We're going to have to lead them off a piece—to the yonder side of the creek," Remington said, making a quick study of the area. "Open ground over there—sort of a field. It won't be hard to stampede them." He paused, shifting his eyes back to the spur of the grove. "Expect I'd first better see what that bunch's doing. Wait here."

Sam moved off at a fast walk, circling the big cottonwood, crouching low as he made his way along an irregular row of prickly gooseberry bushes. Reaching the end of the hedge, Remington dropped to his knees, and near flat to the ground, peered toward the grove.

Willie Vaughn was on his feet, arms folded across his chest as he stared off onto the slope beyond the coach. He was watching the area where his brother and the rest of the outlaw gang would appear.

Sam frowned as quick alarm raced through him. Had Willie heard oncoming horses which he figured would be Jake and his followers?

Remington listened, straining to pick up the beat of hoofs. He could detect nothing; the only sound breaking the hush that blanketed the land was the persistent meadow larks and the distant moaning of a dove. Willie was only hoping, he guessed.

Hank and Dogie were off to one side. Squatting on their heels, they were playing a game of matching coins—flipping coppers up with a thumb, catching them on the back of a hand, and then making a comparison. Charlie, slouched against a tree, was idly whittling at a stick while he puffed at a cigarette. All were turned from him, Sam noted with satisfaction. Drawing back, he got to his feet, and still crouched, hurried to where Longwell awaited him.

"They're all busy doing something or other," he said. "Let's get it done," and continued on to the horses.

He wished he was carrying his belt knife. It would be a good thing to slash the saddle cinches and thereby further delay the outlaws once they had recovered their mounts. But he had laid it aside years ago, finding he never had any use for it. Instead he had only a small pocket knife which he employed for the purpose of halving the apples he bought now and then to treat his favorite horses.

They reached the creek. Remington pointed to a small buckskin and a black to his left. "Pull the ropes loose, then grab the lines. I'll take care of the bay and the chestnut."

Longwell signified his understanding, stepped up to the two horses, freed them, and gathering in the reins, waited while Sam released the others. Then, together, they stepped down into the cool, ankle deep water of the stream, leading the animals through it and the wall of brush lining its opposite bank.

Immediately they broke out onto a long, grassy swale that extended, like a green-floored, tree-walled corridor for a good mile before the cottonwoods closed in once more.

Remington halted, and turning to his horses, hooked the reins behind the saddle horns, motioning for the jurist to do the same. He did not want any of the mounts stepping on a trailing line and coming to a stop.

"All right," he said when Longwell had concluded the chore. His voice was taut and he was hurrying everything—the possibility of Jake Vaughn showing up before they could carry out the remainder of his plan hanging over him like a dark, threatening cloud.

"We start them running—down the swale. Use some rocks, anything. Soon as we get them going, we light out for the stage—same way we come. Don't go bumping into Willie and them—and don't do any yelling!"

Longwell reached down and picked up several clods of dirt and small rocks. "Anytime," he murmured.

Sam, also gathering in a handful of missiles, released his hold on the chestnut and slapped the big gelding smartly on the rump. The horse, startled, leaped forward and broke into a trot.

In that same moment Longwell sent the buckskin he was tending lunging out onto the smooth floor of the swale; then he pivoted, starting his other charge after him. The three horses suddenly bolting was too much for the bay standing near Remington. He sprang forward, setting out at a run after the others.

Sam and Longwell began to hurl the clods and rocks they had accumulated. Few missed at such close range and shortly the four animals were pounding off toward the distant cottonwoods, the sound of their hoofs setting up a rapid drumming in the hush.

A faint yell came from the direction of the outlaws, and as Sam and the judge wheeled and began to retreat into the brush, an exasperated voice carried to them.

"Them damn horses—they've busted loose! Something's spooked them!"

"Get after them!" There was no mistaking Willie Vaughn's shout.

Remington, running low and as fast as his aching leg muscles and short wind would permit, glanced at John Longwell, an arm's length to the side.

"They sure took the bait," he said with a grim smile. "Just keep hoping they don't figure there's a hook in it somewhere."

15

Sucking hard for wind Remington and Longwell reached the last stand of brush beyond which stood the stagecoach. They could hear the outlaws shouting back and forth, and although they were not visible to them, the sound of their voices indicated they had reached the creek, beginning to search about for signs of the missing horses.

"Get aboard—quick!" Sam said as they broke clear of the rabbitbush and hurried toward the team.

Swinging away from the judge, he angled for the front of the coach. The horses were stirring, lifting their heads expectantly as if sensing departure.

Sam took no time to check the hitch and make certain all was ready. There was not a moment to spare. One of the outlaws could suddenly realize their prisoners had been left unguarded and turn back, leaving it to the others to retrieve their straying horses.

Mounting a wheel hub, Remington fairly threw himself onto the seat. It required only seconds to free the lines from the handrail and string them. He did not look down to see if Longwell had entered the coach—he simply took it for granted—and lifting the reins, shook them sharply over the backs of the horses and kicked off the brake.

"Hi–Prince–Brownie!" he called in a low shout. "Move out! Move out!"

The team, nervously shifting in their traces, sprang forward at once. Remington cut hard right to swing the coach about. Instantly a yell went up from somewhere along the creek–Willie Vaughn's voice. They had been seen.

"Hiyah–Dave! Curly! Runner! Dandy!"

Again Remington popped the reins. The six-up leaped ahead almost upsetting the stage as it all but jackknifed in the short arc of the turn.

Abruptly a gunshot cracked through the confusion of dust, jingling harness, and creaking of the coach. Wood splintered off the edge of the seat only inches from Sam Remington's leg. He cursed and hunched lower.

"The horses! Shoot one of the horses!"

The others had now joined Willie Vaughn, Sam realized, as he struggled to get the stagecoach turned to where its bulk would block the outlaws' view of the team. If they succeeded in dropping one of the horses it would be all over–almost before it had begun.

More guns were racketing. The outlaws were running toward them, abandoning for the time their lost mounts. Sam cast a worried glance over his shoulder. They were coming up fast, shooting as they did. Fortunately their hurrying was hindering accuracy.

The coach was broadside to them, and swinging fully around, it would soon present only its narrow rear as a target. It gained that advantage in the next instant, and the six-up now hidden behind it, lengthened into full stride.

No longer were they an easy target for the outlaws. Sam Remington, keeping low, breathed a bit deeper. At least he'd gotten the team safely underway. The horses were the all important thing in those critical moments. The chances of escaping Vaughn and his bunch now were good.

Another slug ripped into the dashboard at Sam's feet, sending up a shower of dust and wood fragments. He heard Longwell say something in a strained voice but the words were lost to him in the noise of the running horses and the rocking, jolting coach.

He looked ahead. The end of the grove was near. Another few yards and they would round the last of the trees and be gone from sight of Willie and the others. If luck would only ride with them for another few seconds they would make it—at least, insofar as Willie and his part of the outlaw gang were concerned.

Jake and the rest were something else. Coming up from Springerville, they would be on the same road. They could be close by—or they could still be miles away; he could only guess which, and pray the latter was true.

But it would be foolish to head back for Apache Springs. Willie and his friends would recover their horses without too much delay, and by cutting across country, intercept them before they could reach the stage depot.

The best bet was, as he'd figured all along, Halverson's way station. It was not too much farther to it. He would just have to gamble on Jake and his bunch being on beyond it. If it turned out the outlaws were in between the grove and the way station he'd be faced with another problem—but he'd cross that river if and when he came to it.

The leaders had reached the end of the grove, beginning to make the turn and head for the road. Back to the rear the outlaws had stopped shooting, evidently deciding they could not halt the stagecoach with bullets, that it would be smarter to recover their mounts and set out in pursuit. . . . Let them, Sam thought. By the time they could get into the saddle his team would be well on the way to Halverson's.

The slight embankment marking the shoulder of the road appeared suddenly above the grass and weeds. The leaders slowed. The remaining horses eased up in their headlong run.

"Brownie—Prince! Get along!" Remington shouted and slapped with the reins.

The team responded blindly, going up over the ledge in a plunging stride as loose dust boiled out from beneath their hoofs and laid a curtain around them.

The front wheels of the stagecoach struck with a thud. The vehicle bounced high, almost throwing Sam off the seat, and slewed dangerously half about. It paused, tipped up onto two wheels, and as muffled screams came from its interior, righted itself and lurched on.

Keeping hard right, Remington continued to veer the horses as they entered the road, ignoring as best he could the rocking and whipping of the coach. The rear wheels came up to meet the ledge. The coach again bounded into the air, reeling sickeningly as it popped and cracked and more dust swirled about it.

Remington, gauging every motion as well as each moment, allowed the heavy vehicle to settle and roll forward briefly, and then cut the team to right angles. The coach snapped about, again poised for a long, breathless moment on two wheels, rocked back onto all four, and then leveled off as the horses strung out in an arrow-straight line.

Remington, sweat dripping from his chin, swore softly. There'd been a couple of near upsets, but he'd managed to get through them without losing any time. Now, if he could reach Halverson's without running smack into Jake

Vaughn and his bunch of cutthroats it would be all over and done with.

He looked ahead. The horses were running full out—ears flat, necks stretched as they pounded along the road, and rolling free behind them, no worse off after the stretch of rough going, was the stage.

Involuntarily Remington looked over his shoulder. The outlaws could not possibly have recovered their horses and begun a pursuit as yet but he felt a need to be sure. There was no one in sight, just as the road leading out before them was empty. He settled back, satisfied. He could figure on at least a quarter hour, perhaps more, before Willie Vaughn and those siding him could start the chase.

Sam Remington turned, cocked his head to one side in order to hear better. Someone was pounding on the side of the coach below him. He leaned over and turned his attention to that point. The strained, white face of Sophie Longwell was staring up at him.

"The judge!" she cried above the whirring wheels and the drumming of the horses. "He's been shot—bad! Please stop—I need help!"

16

Longwell—shot!

Remington groaned. There was no time to pull up—not with Jake Vaughn and his half of the outlaw gang somewhere in front of them, and brother Willie with the rest soon to be at their heels. But he reckoned he had no choice.

Hauling back on the lines, he began to slow the racing team, gradually applying greater pressure while bearing down on the brake until finally the coach came to a stop. Securing the reins and brake, he dropped from the seat and hurriedly opened the door.

The judge was sprawled face down on the forward seat. A broad stain of blood had spread across his back. Sophie was endeavoring to remove the man's coat while, opposite, Stacey Blackburn was again holding the head of the still unconscious Travis on her lap and keeping a wet cloth pressed to his wound.

Sophie glanced around as Sam jerked back the door. "His coat—help me get it off. I must try to stop the bleeding."

Remington crowded into the stage, and bending over John Longwell, lifted him sufficiently for Sophie to remove the outer garment. That out of the way, she ripped the sodden, stained white shirt he was wearing down its center and pushed aside the equally blood-soaked undershirt that was beneath it.

Wordless, totally efficient, the elderly woman then took up a strip of the white cloth earlier provided by either Stacey Blackburn or herself, folded it into a thick pad. Dousing it with water from the canteen, she placed it on the ragged, seeping wound in the jurist's back.

"How'd it happen?" Remington asked. "Last I seen of the judge he was all right."

"Hold this," Sophie directed and reached for another strip of cloth. "When we were turning around and they started shooting at us bullets hit the side of the coach. One barely missed Mrs. Blackburn—it's there in the wood right above her head. We could hear others going right on through the windows. John yelled for us to get down—pushed me off the seat onto the floor.

"Mrs. Blackburn couldn't move her husband. She just stayed where she was. When the bullet almost struck her John stood up and blocked the windows with his body so none of us would get hit. One of them went into his back."

Sam watched the woman take the bit of cloth, rip it into one of length, and passing it under her husband's body, bring it completely around until it encircled him. She then tied it tightly over the pad to form an effective compress. Finished, Sophie then sank back, brushed at the sweat collected on her upper lip. She appeared very old—and tired.

Remington smiled at her. "What the judge done—it took a lot of nerve."

Mrs. Longwell nodded wearily. "I hope he doesn't die from it. Everything seems so senseless—so useless."

Sam glanced off down the road. There was still no sign

of the outlaws—in either direction. "Can I help you with anything else? Best we keep moving—"

"No, that's all we can do for now. How far are we from the way station? John—and Mr. Blackburn—need medicine—a doctor, really."

"We're about eight miles or so from Halverson's," Remington replied, backing out of the coach. "Won't be no doctor there but Dave Halverson's missus is pretty good at it. She'll be able to fix them both up so's they can go on to Springerville."

If we make it to Halverson's, Sam amended silently. Anything could happen during that intervening eight miles of road. Closing the door, he pivoted and stepped quickly to the rear of the stage. Jerking back the boot cover, he dug out his suitcase from the rest of the baggage. Opening it, he obtained his belt and gun and strapped it around his waist.

He immediately felt better with it on although he'd had no use for it in years. Restoring the boot cover, Sam headed toward the front of the coach, pausing at its door. The Blackburns had not changed their positions—the girl, face pale and set with her husband stretched out as best the seat's length would permit, head cushioned on her lap while she held the wet pad to its injured area.

Judge Longwell lay face down, half on, half off the opposite seat, it's width also restricting his position. Sophie Longwell crouched on the floor beside him, features stolid and gray, eyes filled with a remoteness as she absently stroked his hair. She had taken her shawl and draped it over his back and shoulders.

"I'll get you to Halverson's quick as I can, ladies," he said, hoping in the same moment that he could make good on his promise, and hurrying on, climbed back onto the box.

The delay had cost them a good ten minutes, he realized, but there had been no avoiding it—and ten minutes where Willie Vaughn was concerned could mean the difference in reaching or not reaching the way station safely.

Gathering up the reins Remington again threw a glance to the rear. No sign of the outlaws yet. He nodded in satisfaction, kicked off the brake, and slapping the lines, shouted the restive team into motion once more.

They were in an area where the road cut through the heart of the higher hills, one of dips and grades, some short, others lengthy and a few that were fairly steep—these being one of the reasons for a six-horse hitch drawing the stage.

At that moment they were on the crest of one of the higher rises, beginning the long, down-slope run. The team, earlier showing evidence of weariness after the hard pace Billy McElroy had put them through, seemed now to have recovered and were taking the climbs with no apparent effort.

But such was their lot; they had been trained for that specific purpose and knew instinctively what was expected of them, just as they also knew their labor would end at Halverson's, and that the way station was only a few miles farther on.

Billy McElroy . . . Sam's thoughts returned to the young driver as the coach rushed on through the warm, late morning. It was too bad the boy had met his death under such circumstances; he had spent his life for nothing. It was unfortunate, too, that it had not been possible to stop and recover his body for a decent burial. He'd get Halverson to send a buckboard and a couple of men for McElroy; the coyotes and buzzards would leave it untouched for a while yet.

Jeremiah Crenshaw and the Valley Stage Lines would need to find a replacement driver. He'd telegraph the word to the head office when he got to Springerville. It would be up to him, he supposed, to take the stage on into that point from Halverson's as there'd be no driver there who could take over.

No matter—and he really didn't mind. Sitting up there on the box—the wind in his face, the oily feel of leather between his fingers, the song of the wheels in his ears while the horses raced on full out for him—was as natural to Sam Remington as breathing.

In a way he reckoned he was sort of lucky; he'd been granted, through a tragic accident, a reprieve from the retirement that had been thrust upon him; he was being allowed a final opportunity to feel the tug of the lines of his favorite team before withdrawing from the only way of life he'd ever known.

It was a strange way to end his career as a driver. During all the time he'd driven for Valley Lines there'd been no trouble of consequence—an unruly drunk, perhaps, a woman birthing a baby, injured cowhands to be taken to Springerville, lawmen escorting prisoners—never anything more serious than that.

Now, on this final run he had encountered violence at its worst. His successor on the box had been killed, outlaws had taken possession of the coach resulting in two of the passengers being critically injured; and he was making a mad dash to reach Halverson's before those same outlaws, closing in from two sides, could take over again.

That thought reminded Sam once more of Willie Vaughn. He twisted about, gave the dust-clouded road behind the stage another careful study. The outlaws had yet to put in their appearance; evidently they had had difficulty in recovering their horses.

His mind switched then to his passengers. Spreading his legs wide and bracing himself with his feet, he leaned over the side of the seat.

"Everything all right in there?" he shouted above noise of the speeding coach.

"All right." Sophie Longwell's faint reply was barely audible.

"Good. Not much farther now," Remington said and straightened up on the box.

A few miles, mostly all hills, and they'd be at the way station. He hoped Sarah Halverson would be on hand and not off visiting family as she sometimes was. Longwell and Travis Blackburn needed all the help they could get.

He'd best figure on a delay at the way station. Two, perhaps three hours instead of the usual one. Both men, once Sarah had done what she could for them, would need rest and quiet. That didn't matter either; he was the only one aboard now that would be interested in making connections with another stage, and that wasn't important. He could easily catch a later one—in fact if Sarah Halverson felt it was necessary they could lay over until morning.

Too, he would need help, recruit men to ride shotgun for him. It would take several, in fact, to keep the Vaughn gang at a safe distance if they were to continue on. . . . Sam Remington, staring ahead, drew up slowly. His eyes had caught a glimpse of riders topping out a distant hill. Five men—indistinct figures silhouetted on the horizon some two miles or less away.

He swore feelingly. It could only be Jake Vaughn and his followers—and Halverson's was on beyond them.

17

Remington's jaw tightened. They were trapped, caught between Jake Vaughn and his party approaching from the south, and brother Willie with his three hard-case friends who shortly would be coming in from the north.

It was useless to waste time searching for a place to hide. There was only the road with its weedy shoulders and here in this particular section the pines were thinly scattered and offered no refuge.

He doubted that Jake Vaughn or any of the men riding with him had spotted the coach. It had been well down on the slope they had just topped, and consequently had not been outlined against the sky as were the outlaws. There was still time to do something if he could come up with a practical idea.

Skull Pass. . . . The road leading to it lay a quarter mile or so on ahead, cutting off to the left and climbing to the not too far crest of Skull Ridge in the east. But could the team manage it? Once the route used by wagons and stagecoaches traveling from Springerville to Apache Springs, it had been abandoned many years back when the easier, more circuitous route through the Whiskey Mountains, which eliminated the steep climbs and dangerous switchbacks, was constructed. He wasn't too familiar with the road, having been over it only once and then on horseback, but in it Sam Remington was seeing a way out.

He'd have to make the decision soon. To take it meant rough, hard going for his passengers, two of whom were critically wounded; and there was the possibility they'd not get through at all—ending up wrecked somewhere along the tortuous trail or halted against a landslide that blocked passage. In either event the possibility that John Longwell and Travis Blackburn would die could be considered a foregone conclusion.

But to stay where they were and again become prisoners of the Vaughn brothers and their outlaw gang meant certain death also—not only for the man they were determined to lynch, but for all who would bear witness to their vengeance as well.

Still—it could be that Jake, not actually aware that Longwell was aboard, would not attempt to halt the coach. Like as not he'd be thinking that Willie was holding the judge captive back in the grove, as planned.

Remington shrugged. That was only wishful thinking. As carefully as the activities of Longwell had been looked into by the Vaughns, Jake would know the only stage on the road that day would be the one carrying the jurist. And since the plan had been to hold it and its occupants prisoner until he arrived, he'd guess at once that something had misfired and Willie had permitted it to slip through his fingers and act accordingly. No, there'd be no getting by Jake Vaughn.

The faint ruts of the Skull Pass road came into view on his left. Sam threw a glance to the north. Tension lifted within him. Willie Vaughn and his three followers were now in sight—a long mile or so back—but coming on. That completed it; the outlaws had him boxed in unless—

Sam Remington debated the matter with himself no longer. There was a slim chance he could get the stage and his passengers through to Springerville by Skull Pass—none at all if he remained on the main road. Hauling in on the lines he slowed the team, and when the leaders drew abreast the worn grooves, now overgrown with grass and short weeds, he swung the team sharp left.

The coach jolted and rocked as it came off the shoulder and Remington thought he heard a moan of pain coming from its interior but he did not slow. The first half mile or so up the valley-like approach to the pass was open country, devoid of all but grass and a few barrel-sized clumps of brush, where the stage would be clearly visible. There was a scatter of trees, however, in the near distance that would screen them for a brief stop.

The horses, straining on the slight grade, continued at a fair pace while Remington anxiously kept a watch on the road behind them for the outlaws. Willie Vaughn and his party should reach the point where he had turned off first since they had been the nearest.

With luck—which so far hadn't favored him greatly, Remington thought ruefully—the outlaws would not notice the wheel prints cutting away from the main route, and would ride on by and continue until they met Jake and the others.

They would quickly backtrack then, figuring the coach had to be somewhere along the way—pulled off to the side, perhaps. But by that moment Sam intended to have the stage through Skull Pass and descending its far side.

They reached the trees and swung in behind them. With the horses blowing hard from their efforts, Remington secured the lines and brake, climbed down and hurriedly opened the door of the coach.

"Why–" Sophie Longwell began and broke off as Sam raised a hand and silenced her.

Speaking fast he explained the situation–that they were caught between the two outlaw parties, and that he had made the decision to risk the old Skull Pass route rather than permit them to all become prisoners again.

"We ain't got a prayer if they get their hands on us–you know that," he said. "And we're not much better off doing this–far as staying alive's concerned. But at least, we'll stand a chance."

"Will we be able to get through?" Sophie asked, frowning. "I know these old abandoned roads are usually–"

"I can't answer that right off," Remington replied. "I expect there'll be plenty of bad sections, most of which we'll be able to manage. The thing that could stop us is a washout or a place where the rocks've slid down and blocked the way."

Remington glanced at Stacey Blackburn for her comment. She seemed lost, voiceless. Travis was still unconscious, motionless on her lap as a man dead.

"I don't think my husband can stand any rough traveling," Sophie Longwell continued. "Mr. Blackburn either. I'm not sure we're doing the right thing."

Sam impatiently swung his attention to the main road. He could not see it from where they were but by that time Willie Vaughn and his men were likely near the point where he'd turned off.

"I don't think you understand, ma'am," he said politely, coming back to the elderly woman. "There just ain't nothing else we can do."

"But John–Mr. Blackburn–they won't survive–"

Longwell stirred weakly. "It's our only hope, Sophie," he murmured. "Remington knows what's best."

"Can't we just stay here and wait until they've gone

on?" Stacey, rousing finally, asked. "The trees are hiding us."

"Yes," Sophie put in quickly. "They can't see us, and once they've gone on we could return to the main road and be on our way."

"It won't work out like that," Remington explained. "They'll get together—maybe already have—and figure they've overshot us. Right then they'll double back and start looking for tracks. There's nine of them—enough to spread out and cover the ground good. It won't take them long to find out we headed for Skull Pass and start after us."

"Then there's really not much use in trying to escape this way—"

"Odds are sure better'n staying on that road. We get into the rough country on the other side of the ridge, there'll be plenty of places where we can pull off and hide if we have to. And it's a lot shorter to Springerville, too—by several miles.

"My feeling is that we can make it—or leastwise get close enough to where that bunch'll be scared to jump us. There's usually folks traveling the main road, once we get on it."

Again Sam Remington glanced over his shoulder. Urgency was pushing him relentlessly. The climb to the pass from where they had halted would be no easy one and they should get underway. Their chances of reaching Springerville without the outlaws overtaking them would improve considerably, too, if they could gain the far side of the ridge before the outlaws discovered the course they had followed.

By God, he'd not wait any longer. The decision was his, anyway. He was in charge—not the passengers. He'd make it and stand by it. Sam stepped back and started to turn away; he paused as John Longwell's faltering voice reached him.

"Go ahead, Remington," the judge said. He still lay face down on the seat in deference to the wound in his back. "I'm sure Blackburn would tell you the same if he was able. Better to risk a bad road than just hand ourselves over to the Vaughns."

"I agree," Stacey said unexpectedly.

Sophie Longwell sighed and made a slight adjustment of the compress placed over her husband's wound. Close by, in the cluster of squat cedar trees behind which they had stopped, a scrub jay scolded noisily.

"I suppose it's all we can do," the woman said.

"Yes'm, it sure is," Remington replied, and closing the door, he wheeled to make a quick check of the team.

The horses were benefiting from the short rest and as he moved alongside them, examining the harness, making certain all was in place and secure, he talked steadily to them in quiet voice.

They were facing a hard chore. Ordinarily their day's work would be over by this time, having reached Halverson's where another six-up would take their place. Instead they would be called on to continue pulling the coach over a much more difficult and trying stretch of country, and at the best speed of which they were capable.

He'd have to husband them carefully, Sam knew: conserve their strength at every opportunity, avoid the steep grades whenever possible and breathe them at every opportunity. Tired already, in need of water, they had their work cut out for them—just as he had his.

The harness was all in proper set and there was nothing to be gained in allowing them to rest any longer. First, however, he'd like an idea of where they stood in relation to the outlaws. If the Vaughns hadn't discovered that he'd swung the coach onto the Skull Pass road, it wouldn't be necessary to press the team in its climb to the pass; if the opposite was true and they were now coming up the narrow valley in pursuit, he'd have to call on the horses for every bit of speed they could muster.

Dropping back, Remington trotted to the edge of the cedars, disturbing several more blue and gray jays in the process, and reached a point where he could see the road. A grunt of relief escaped his tight lips. There were no riders in the little valley. The Vaughns had not yet discovered that he had tricked them.

Reversing himself, Sam hurried back to the coach and climbed to his perch. Gathering up the lines and releasing the brake, he swung the team about and pointed for Skull Pass—a sharp gash in the ragged line of the distant ridge.

He'd keep the trees between the coach and the road for as long as possible; when the outlaws finally learned of what he had done they would not have found it out by seeing the stage ascending the grade but from the slower process of ferreting out the tracks left by the coach and its team.

18

The going was smooth if somewhat steep. Thick grass covered the slope and it was not until they were drawing near the crest that they began to encounter loose rocks scattered about as well as others half buried in the dark soil. Sam Remington skillfully guided the coach around all such obstructions, sparing not only the injured men pain and discomfort, but also avoiding possible hurt to his team and damage to the stage.

They gained the pass, rolling through its narrow confines with no difficulty. From that high vantage point Remington, allowing the horses to walk slow, turned his eyes back to the Apache Springs-Springerville highway, now in the distance. Hope rose within him. There was no one in sight. Apparently the outlaws were still searching for them.

He came back to the job at hand. The old trail, rutted and more distinct as it laid its way across the barren summit of Skull Ridge than it had been on the grass-covered slope, cut sharp right at the end of the pass, where it began a descent across the west wall of a deep canyon. It was in such places as this they could expect to meet trouble, Sam knew, as he threw his glance ahead.

Storms that periodically ripped through the high hill

country often dislodged boulders, sending them crashing down to block a road. And wild, roaring arroyos filled with slashing, turbulent water also often left their mark in impassable gashes. He saw no evidence of these yet, but his probing gaze was limited only to the first bend.

The horses, despite the long pull, seemed affected little—a testimonial to their strength—but Remington himself was now beginning to feel the drag on his body. The tight control he was forced to exercise over the team, the careful handling of the coach, and the total weight of responsibility were combining to wear him down.

On the well-defined, familiar, and trouble-free course connecting the two settlements he would have, by that hour, become aware of only a mild weariness, a gentle reminder that he was no longer as young as he was once. It would have bothered him not at all; any man grew tired on his job at the end of the day.

However, negotiating the narrow, rough trail that whipped across the face of the canyon, all the while striving to conserve the horses, spare his wounded passengers as much pain as possible, and still put as much ground between the outlaws and the stagecoach as he could, was a different matter.

He raised a hand to brush at the sweat beading his forehead. They were making slow progress. Rocks, fortunately of no large sizes, littered the road and washed out places, and chuck holes were numerous although none were deep enough to present a serious problem.

A ragged hogback, like a chalk-white band, now towered over them as they slowly dropped lower toward the floor of the canyon. He could not see, nor could he recall what course the road took once they reached that level, but it seemed to him that it followed the brush-filled, sandy bottom for a short distance and then began to ascend the opposite wall.

It appeared the road had not been used by anyone in some time. There were no wheel tracks or prints of horses hoofs to be seen, but Remington knew that was not absolute proof; one hard rainstorm would obliterate all traces of another's passage in but a few minutes, and there had been rain recently. He could see dark, damp places beneath overhanging ledges and occasionally he noted the wrinkled surface of where there had been a pool only lately sucked dry by the sun.

Abruptly they came off the canyon wall and were on its floor. Remington frowned. The road had disappeared, the ruts that marked it having been wiped clean. But the natural course, since the opposing canyon wall now lifted before him in a sheer, perpendicular palisade with no indication of even a deer trail, was logically on down the bottom of the deep gorge. Accordingly, he continued in that direction.

Progress now was slow for a different reason. Where before they had been crossing a firm, if rough, surface, the horses were now bucking loose sand, with clumps of Apache plume, doveweed, and other springy growth barring their way constantly. Large rocks also blocked the wash occasionally and time after time Sam Remington was forced to halt, back a necessary distance, and swing wide to get past an obstacle.

Shortly he brought the team to a halt, choosing an island-like patch of gravelly ground upon which to stop so that the winded horses would have no difficulty in moving on after they had rested. Dismounting he first saw to the sweating, blowing team, again making a quick but thorough check of the harness, and then dropped back to the coach for a look at his passengers.

John Longwell had fared badly. The rocking and jolting had started his wound bleeding again. Travis Blackburn, still mercifully unconscious, was unchanged.

"Are we anywhere near the town?" Sophie Longwell asked in an exhausted voice.

Remington shook his head. "Afraid we're only about half way through the mountains—if that much."

The woman sighed. "I don't think my husband can stand much more," she said worriedly.

"I'm taking it easy as I can—"

"I know," Sophie broke in hurriedly. "I'm not blaming you—and I know this is the only thing we could do. I—I just hope we can get to that town soon."

Longwell raised his head slightly. "Don't fret, Sophie. I'll be all right."

Sam shifted his attention to Stacey Blackburn. "Your man no better?"

The girl managed a weak smile. "He came to once—back there where the road was so rough—but it was only for a moment. Have you seen any sign of the outlaws?"

Remington drew back, glancing toward the rim of the canyon. Skull Pass was not visible from where he stood, his view being barred by the curvature of the land and the bulging shoulders of rock; nor was the higher region of the road where it snaked back and forth across the face of the slope.

"Not so far, I haven't," he replied. "Could be we're going to get lucky."

Sam wheeled at that, walked slowly back to the front of the stage and climbed tiredly up onto the box. His shoulders and arms were protesting every move he made and his legs were trembling. He brushed at his mouth nervously; a drink from that bottle of whiskey Dogie had produced back at the grove would be worth a double eagle, he thought; even a swallow of water would help, but he reckoned his thirst could not be as great as that of the team.

Remington sat quiet, delayed another five minutes to give the horses as much rest as possible, and then shaking out the lines and releasing the brake, he started them forward. The coach began to roll on the solid ground easily, but slowed abruptly as the wheels, leaving the graveled surface, dropped off into the loose sand. They sank deep, immediately throwing a heavy load on the team, but the horses, digging in hard and fighting for every step, continued on their way.

Without warning a covey of quail exploded almost from under the hoofs of the off leader, Prince, and thundered off into the sky like small, blue shooting stars. The wiry chestnut came up on his hind legs, threw himself to one side, and started to fall. Instantly the team was in frantic confusion with Sam Remington standing upright working with the reins, struggling to control the wildly plunging horses.

The chestnut recovered himself and he swung back into line, but the forward motion of the heavy stagecoach was lost and the iron-tired wheels had sunk deeper into the seemingly bottomless sand.

"Brownie! Prince!" Remington shouted, dashing the sweat from his eyes with a forearm. "Go! Curly! Dandy! Hiyah! Hiyah! Getalong!"

The horses responded valiantly, lunging against their collars, striving to break the ponderous drag of the coach.

"Hiyah—Dave! Runner!"

Remington heard Sophie Longwell call out something but ignored whatever it was. He could see the beginning of the road, where it left the arroyo and began the ascent of the east slope of the canyon only yards away. If he could keep the horses moving, even if only inches at a time, and prevent their suddenly laying back in the harness, they would shortly reach solid footing.

"Dave—Brownie! Pull, damn you—pull!"

The team fought on, hoofs thudding, metal jingling, the coach creaking and groaning as dust boiled about it. The lead horses came to the edge of the wash. Unhesitating, they lunged up and onto the firm clay surface. The swing team followed, crowding the hindquarters of the leaders. A moment later the wheel horses, their powerful legs driving iron-shod hoofs into the slack sand like steam pistons, were out of the wash and dragging the coach up the slight slope and onto the trail.

Remington, every muscle in his arms and shoulders screaming their complaint, sank back onto the seat. He allowed the team to surge on, gain the summit of a rise a dozen wheel turns from the arroyo, and there drew them in. As they came to a halt, shaking their heads, trembling, blowing hard, he swore at them affectionately. How they were able to do it after the long, hard day that they had already put in he found impossible to understand.

They deserved, and would get a rest now; he was only sorry there was no water to give them after they had cooled, but there was no help there; the wash was bone dry and they would have to wait until later. Anchoring the lines, Sam turned to climb down. He'd best go over the harness carefully; the strain thrown on the leather had been severe.

He froze, eyes on the road; now visible to him were nine riders making the descent. . . . The outlaws had found their tracks, spotted the coach on the floor of the canyon, and were closing in.

19

Eyes narrowed, Remington studied the distant riders. They were in single file and descending at a fast pace. In a very short while they would reach the floor of the canyon. Grim, he swung his attention back to the indistinct traces of the road ahead as it angled up that side of the deep cleft.

They were facing a hard pull with a team that was tired, if willing. The odds were a hundred to one that his horses could outrun those of the outlaws, but there did appear to be many off-shoot canyons into which he could take the coach. That was no answer, he realized in the next moment; sooner or later they would be found.

"Please—can't we hurry! My husband—"

Sophie Longwell's plaintive voice reached him again, and once more he ignored it. He was doing all he could. . . . There was no choice but to continue, hope that something would turn up, and failing that, make a stand. With one gun against nine, however, resistance on his part would be short-lived.

He decided to forego checking the harness and the horses; likely all was still in order and it was foolish to delay any further. Taking up the lines, he put the six-up into motion and began the climb. The team moved slowly, the two or three minutes' rest they had gained during the brief stop accomplishing little more than allowing them to catch their breath.

He supposed he should have taken time to advise the passengers of the outlaws' reappearance to keep them informed of the serious situation they were up against, but in the press of urgency he hadn't thought of it. Probably just as well, he concluded. There was nothing the women could do, and the men were out of it. The responsibility to cope with the matter was all his.

He saw no more of the oncoming outlaws as intervening trees now blocked off all view of the opposite side of the canyon, but as they continued up the incline at a steady trot, he nevertheless maintained a close watch on the general area behind them.

They rounded a bend, and the road flattened out perceptibly. At once the horses increased their pace. Although there were little more than worn ruts to mark the route, the going was much easier here than Sam had anticipated. He supposed it was because water from the severe rainstorms drained at a more gradual rate down the branch canyons and washes of the long slope they were climbing than the one opposite which was much more precipitous.

Remington's gaze halted on the mouth of a narrow, valley-like swale to his left. Floored with grass, studded with rocks and the expected number of pine and other trees, it was nevertheless different from others he'd noted in that he could see a horizon in the not too far distance. That summit, he realized, was the east rim of the Whiskey Mountains.

An idea born of desperation spurted into Sam Remington's beleaguered mind. Springerville lay beyond that rim—just exactly where he was not certain—but it was in that direction. If he swung the stagecoach off the road they were now following and managed to get it to that crest and descend to the plain below, they would throw the outlaws off their trail and be able to continue on to the settlement unmolested.

But he would be gambling on what he would face once they made it to the rim; it could be a cliff, a palisade down which it would be impossible to take the team and coach—or it could offer a sloping route no worse than that traveled after pulling through Skull Pass.

As he saw it, the odds were even. At the worst, he'd find himself at a dead end—which was what they would be up against if they continued along the road they were now pursuing—a dead end created by the outlaws who surely would soon overtake them.

Again the decision was his—and he made it. Abruptly Remington slowed the team, and veering away from the ruts, headed into the narrow canyon. He permitted the horses to proceed for a hundred feet or so and then brought them to a halt.

Immediately he heard Sophie Longwell's questioning voice again, once more ignored it, and dropping to the ground, he hurried to the rear of the coach. Reaching into the boot he obtained the slicker he had noticed earlier—Billy McElroy's he assumed—and quickly doubled back to the road. There, by using the rain garment, he swept out all traces of where the team and stagecoach had departed the route, going so far as to kick several clumps of dead weeds into the area.

That completed, he returned to the stage, pausing here and there on the way to obliterate several indications of the vehicle's passage with the slicker that just might catch one of the outlaw's eye as he did. Sophie, her head and shoulders framed in the window of the door, was waiting for him. He restored the slicker to the boot and faced her.

"They're crowding our heels," he said, making his explanation before she could ask her question. "I aim to head up over that ridge at the top of this canyon. If we're lucky—there'll be a way down the other side."

The woman frowned. "What if there's not?"

"Only thing to do then is have it out with them."

Sophie Longwell sighed hopelessly. "I guess it doesn't really matter," she murmured and settled back.

Remington stepped in closer and glanced inside. The Blackburns were as he'd last seen them—Stacey wedged in a corner of the rear seat, Travis's head on her lap. His skin had a bloodless pallor; the girl's was little different as she returned Sam's gaze with her large, dark eyes.

Judge Longwell, still lying face down, appeared to be sleeping, or like Blackburn, was unconscious. It would be a miracle, Sam thought as he hastily climbed back up onto his perch, if the two men lived through the remainder of the day.

He gathered in the lines, wishing now that he had his whip. When he'd completed his last run back at Apache Springs he'd given the stiff-handled lash to one of the hostlers—and Billy McElroy's had been lost when the young driver had tumbled from his seat. Remington was no believer in using a whip except when training a team, but here, with the horses worn and the worst yet to come, a whip could serve a purpose.

There was, of course, no rutted trail to follow. Sam simply started the team up the long, ascending draw, keeping away from its narrow floor where there was an accumulation of rocks, brush, and other storm-carried debris that would make it more difficult for the horses.

The team proceeded slowly, hoofs alternately slipping on the grass or digging into the firm, rocky soil as they fought their way up the grade. Each time a fairly level plateau was reached, Remington brought them to a halt, allowing them to rest.

Their need for water was critical by that moment, but he could do nothing about it. What little had been in McElroy's canteen had gone to dress the wounds of the injured men. Perhaps, once they gained the summit there would be a creek or a spring where they could slake their thirsts.

They were in no danger of being seen from the road by the outlaws and that made it possible to give the team longer rest breaks. A wealth of trees and shrubs lay behind them, forming an effective screen, and Jake and Willie Vaughn would pass the turn-off point—if they had not already done so—aware of nothing more than the distant horizon, if indeed they even troubled to notice that.

The team labored on, sometimes with Remington at his customary place on the box, other times with him walking alongside one of the leaders, hand on a bridle while he encouraged them each in turn in his firm, familiar voice.

The last few yards were the most difficult of all, being nearly a vertical ledge of granite that all but blocked their way. Sam, however, by rolling aside several rocks, created a narrow aisle up which he led the team.

Clearing the path required a full half hour in which they accomplished little more than a half a dozen yards. Once Prince, the off leader, fell and there were moments when the coach teetered dangerously, but finally they were on the crest and moving along a flinty saddle for the opposite side.

Gaining that point, Remington, on foot as he brought the team up and across that final leg of the climb, pulled to a halt at the edge and surveyed the country far below.

Well to the south smoke hung in the clear sky. That

would be Springerville, and out on the long-reaching, brushy flat to the east, a ribbon of brown could be seen threading toward it—the main road connecting the town with points north, Remington realized. All they need do was get off the ridge and onto it, and the drive into Springerville would be a lark.

Sober, Sam Remington turned his attention then to the slope dropping away from beneath his feet. That would be the problem—getting down to the flat. The grade was near perpendicular. Keeping a team from falling and a coach from overturning could be considered next to an impossibility.

20

Remington, letting the weary sweat- and dust-caked team stand, walked forward along the rim searching for a place to begin the descent. It had not entered his mind to abandon the idea and turn back; like the charioteers of old he would never give up as long as he had wheels under him and horses to drive.

Within a short distance he came onto a shallow wash, one that drained gently off the plateau and flowed on down the slope. It would not be possible to turn into it from the meadow-like area where they had halted, but by swinging as far right as possible, he could jackknife, approach at right angles, and thereby get off the ridge. From there on he'd be facing the difficulties of descending the long, broken slope to the flat below—but he'd take that as it came.

Pivoting, he returned to the coach. The horses were quiet, not the usual restive animals anxious to be on the move that they ordinarily were, and walking slowly by them he examined their harness closely, making doubly certain there were no loose buckles or snaps that were about to come loose.

Satisfied that all was secure, he turned then to the brake beam. It was clear, with no impeding bits of gravel or dirt that might hinder its operation. The shoes, he recalled, were fairly new having been replaced only a few weeks previous.

That was one bit of luck that came his way. It would be necessary to make liberal use of them once they were off the ridge and headed downgrade; the problem then would not be one of the team pulling the coach but of preventing the coach from running into the team.

"What is it? Can't we make it any farther?"

Sophie Longwell drew him to the side of the stage with her question.

"There's the road," he said, pointing to the narrow trace far out on the flat. "Leads right on in to Springerville. We get on it we're practically there."

The woman nodded, pulled herself closer to the side of the stage, and considered the slope. She shook her head skeptically.

"Are you going to try and drive down that?"

"Only way to get to it. It's either that or the outlaws."

"I know—but is it possible? It looks so steep and rough."

"If Mr. Remington believes he can do it, I expect he can," Stacey Blackburn said from the depths of the coach. "He's got us through safely so far."

Sam smiled wanly. He wished he had some of the girl's confidence; to him it was something that had to be done because there was no alternative. A man would be a damn fool to try it, otherwise.

"I suppose you're right," Sophie said, drawing back.

"It's going to be straight-down going all the way," Remington said then, feeling it best to caution the women. "It'd be best if you could all get out and walk, but we can forget that unless you want to leave your men—"

"No," Stacey said before he could finish.

"I'll stay with my husband, too," Sophie added quickly.

"I figured that. Now, brace yourself the best you can and hang onto something so you won't get bounced around any more than's to be expected. I ain't aiming to turn us over but if it happens, don't get scared. This coach is a strong one and plenty well built. It won't come apart or cave in on you."

Remington moved off, stepped up onto the hub of the front wheel, and took his place on the seat. He'd need to brace himself solidly, too, but with one foot on the brake lever, the other jammed against the dashboard he should be all right—barring any accidents.

Sam brushed that thought from his mind, and taking up the leathers, put the team into motion. He allowed the horses to proceed briefly, then cut them hard right until they were as far back from the edge of the ridge as possible. Reversing course at that point, he cut sharp, circled, and drove them up to where they came onto the wash head-on. There he halted, giving the leaders a chance to see what lay in front of them while he, too, had another long look.

The team, sensing danger, stamped nervously. It would be best not to rush them or force them onto the grade but let them feel their way on their own. By so doing they would have greater confidence in their footing.

Lifting the reins, Remington shook them gently. Immediately the horses moved out. Unhesitating, they stepped off the near level surface of the plateau. Both leaders, heads bobbing, began to hold back as they became aware of the slanting ground beneath them and felt their teammates crowding in behind them. And then as the coach came to the lip, hung briefly in the air and suddenly tipped forward to throw its weight against them, they started down the grade.

Instantly Sam Remington jammed on the brake. The stage steadied and the horses strung out, drawing the harness taut as they leaned into it. Back wheels locked, the coach began to follow along in the boiling dust wake of the horses, laying back on their haunches, hoofs digging deep into the firm soil as they fought to maintain balance and not go plunging headlong down the slope.

The surface became rougher. Jagged rocks, half buried in the dark soil set the coach rocking and creaking alarmingly as wheels thudded into them. Metal clanged loudly as the iron shoes of the horses, struggling to stay upright, came in contact.

Remington, flopping back and forth on the seat like a rag doll, shoulders and arms throbbing from the strain, muscles of his legs screaming in protest, looked ahead. Sweat blanketed his face and misted his eyes but he dared not spare a hand to dash it aside. It was slow going, he saw—terribly slow; they were less than a third of the way down and it appeared that the worst was yet to come.

Dust was now a dark cloud enveloping the horses and coach as they descended. It hung about Sam Remington in a choking, blinding haze but he seemed not to notice it; he merely narrowed his eyes more as he sought to peer through the pall and guide the team as best he could.

Half way . . . Remington crouched, legs braced, feeling a tremor of doubt rushing through him. The team was beginning to wilt under the relentless pressure of the steep descent. Smoke was coming from the brake shoes as they jammed their surfaces against the iron tires of the rear wheels, but their restricting hold appeared to be weakening. And his own strength seemed to be waning, giving rise to the possibility he could not maintain his tight control over team and vehicle much longer.

And then abruptly, an unexpected arroyo slanting down from higher climes barred the way. Remington, lines taut, brake jammed tight, endeavored to slow the downward momentum of his team. The horses were unable to respond. The leaders veered sharply as they approached the narrow, ditch-like cut. The swing horses crowded into them. They in turn felt the sudden collision of the wheels coming into them from behind.

Brownie and Prince reacted instinctively. Both gathered themselves and lunged across the wash. Their teammates followed, dragging the stagecoach in their wake. The front wheels of the vehicle dropped into the gash with a loud rattle of metal and the crackling and groaning of wood, and then rebounded up the opposite side.

The big rear wheels followed, plunging down into the gap with a repeat of the noise and an explosion of dust. The coach rocked from side to side, then pitched sharply to the left. The horses, plunging on, snapped it back around. It slewed wildly and went broadside and up onto two wheels where it teetered breathlessly as screams came from its interior.

Remington, the ominous crackling of wheels in his ears, slapped with the reins. There was but one thing to do—send the horses hard into their collars. The sudden jerk would whip the coach back into line, prevent it from toppling.

"Brownie—Prince—hiyah!" he yelled. "Get!"

The team surged ahead recklessly on the steep slope. The stagecoach swung about, reeled sickeningly, and staggered into place again. Remington, booted foot pressed against the brake, leg rigid despite the cramping that threatened to tear the muscles from calf and thigh, kept his weight against the lines. The horses were fighting him every step, shaking their heads violently as they sought to free themselves from the bit and race unchecked down the grade.

But they slowed, obedient to the steel clamped between their teeth and the insistent voice of their driver; once more they began to dig in. The groaning and creaking of the lurching coach began to fade and shortly, Sam Remington, straining to see through the swirling dust, realized they were at the foot of the slope, that only a gentle dip lay between them and the flat.

Aching, bathed in sweat, so weary he could scarcely hold up his arms, he glanced back at the grade. They had made it. Hauling in on the lines he brought the team to a halt, climbed down from his perch and turned his dust-streaked face to the near window of the coach.

"You folks all right in here?" he asked anxiously.

Sophie Longwell, sprawled across her husband in her efforts to prevent him being tossed about during the wild descent, pulled herself about. Disheveled, hair loose, clothing in disarray, she nodded woodenly. Stacey Blackburn presented a similar appearance, but her face was tear-streaked and her eyes were filled with a deep fear. Blackburn had been thrown from the seat and now lay mostly on the floor although his head was still on the girl's lap.

"We're down," Remington said, opening the door and lifting Travis back to his original position. "We'll be on the road in a few more minutes. Ain't far now to Springerville."

"Thank God," Sophie murmured in a low voice, and then added with rising stress, "Please hurry, will you? I don't think my husband can last much longer."

Sam stepped back and closed the door. "I'll do the best

I can, ma'am. The horses are about down. I've all but run them into the ground—but we'll make it."

"Please—please hurry!"

Remington returned to the box and to the horses, frantic now to break into a run and release the tension that had built up within them during the difficult descent.

But that was all behind them now, he realized thankfully as they turned onto the road—the test thrown to the team, the skill and strength required to handle them, and the danger that had threatened his passengers. They could roll on into Springerville without further worry, hopefully in time for a doctor to help Longwell and Travis Blackburn, and save their lives. Hours had elapsed since they had been injured and there was little doubt in Sam Remington's mind that both men were critical. But the horses had only so much left in them, and despite Sophie Longwell's plea and his own wishes, he was not going to push them past their limit; better to get there late than not at all.

Sam stared ahead. The road was a good one, wide and straight except where the tip of the Whiskey Mountains, off which they had just come, trailed down to meet the flat. There a mass of rocks and brush formed a ragged shoulder and set up a barrier around which the course was forced to curve as it hurried on to reach the town.

He'd be damned glad when this one was over with, Remington thought, slumping on the seat. It would be a relief to pull into the depot, get his passengers taken care of, turn the team over to the hostlers, and then treat himself to a stiff drink.

It had been one hell of a ride—one he'd not forget as long as he lived, and strangely, he was discovering now that it was over, that he'd enjoyed it—every damned minute of the strain and tension. Maybe he ought to forget about quitting, find himself a driving job with another stage line. He was a lot stronger than he'd led himself to believe, and—

Remington came erect, jaw tightening. Riders were moving out from behind the bulge of brush and rocks at the end of the mountain and were forming a line to block his way. Nine men—the Vaughns and their outlaw partners.

21

Anger roared through Sam Remington's weary frame—a burning, frustrated anger that turned him savagely belligerent. After all he'd been through—the time in the grove, the road to Skull Pass and beyond, the short cut down the trackless east side of the mountains on which he'd gambled and won—and now the sonofabitching Vaughns and their crowd were out there waiting.

He might as well have never left the grove of cottonwoods for all the good it had done him and his passengers; all that effort expended in trying to throw the outlaws off their trail had gone for nothing. Instead of searching the draws and canyons for the coach and its passengers when he had tricked them that last time, as he'd figured they would, the outlaws had simply continued along the old road, evidently aware that eventually, he would have to pass that point at the end of the Whiskeys on his way to the settlement.

Well, he wasn't through yet. It was a long two or three miles to Springerville and he had a dog-tired string of horses on his hands, dead game and almost down to their knees for sure, but they would give him all they had left if he asked for it. He'd not give in to the Vaughns, damn them! They'd have to fight him.

Drawing his pistol, Sam laid it on the seat beside him where it would be quickly available, and put his attention on the team. The horses were down to a trot, moving easily, almost mechanically, with the coach rolling freely on the slight grade leading into the town.

He stared moodily ahead, keeping the team at its slow pace as they drew nearer to the outlaws. They had formed a line across the road. He recognized Willie and reckoned the big fellow on a tall bay beside him was brother Jake. They looked somewhat alike. Ranged elsewhere in the irregular string were Hank and Dogie, and the one called Charlie. The others who had come with Jake he did not know.

All were slouched on their saddles, and their grizzled faces in the shadows of their wide-brimmed hats appeared dark and pleased as if gloating over the fact that, after all he had done to sidetrack them, they'd won out anyway.

The team drew nearer, the ears of the lead horses pricking forward questioningly as they saw the barrier in the road that faced them and awaited the pull on the lines that would tell them to stop. But Sam Remington had no such thought; he let them continue their approach, the reins now all in his left hand, sagging loosely over their broad backs.

Twenty yards . . . fifteen. . . . Jake Vaughn raised his arm signaling to halt. The men strung out to either side of him stirred as if nervous. Ten yards . . .

"Hiyah—Brownie! Prince! Dave! Dandy—run!"

The command exploded from Sam Remington's lips suddenly, and snatching up his pistol, he fired point-blank at Jake Vaughn.

The outlaw buckled, almost falling from the saddle as the team drove straight on at the abruptly milling line of riders scrambling to get out of the way. Remington, slapping with the lines, triggered his weapon again, this time in the general direction of the riders, and heard a yelp of pain as the coach swept by them. He had a quick glimpse of Willie Vaughn's taut face, of Hank leaning forward clutching his shoulder, and then the stage had whirled past as the horses settled into an all-out run.

Remington, with the lines still clutched in one hand, his pistol in the other, twisted about and looked back. Five of the outlaws were swinging onto the road and giving chase. The remaining members of the gang—Jake Vaughn and Hank among them—had pulled off to the side. One had dismounted; hastening up to the elder Vaughn, he was evidently intending to assist him from his mount.

Steadying himself as best he could, grim set and fully aware the pursuing outlaws could overtake his spent team with little effort, Sam took aim as best he could with the coach rocking and swaying beneath him, and squeezed off a shot. The bullet missed the mark, but apparently by a narrow margin; one of the riders swerved aside, slowed briefly, and then came on.

The outlaws opened up with their weapons at that point. Sam could not hear the leaden slugs strike but knew some were ripping into the back of the coach, tearing at the canvas boot and dimpling the curved panels. The horses were comparatively safe from bullets, having the bulk of the stage between them and the outlaws, and for that he was grateful. But it wouldn't stay that way unless he succeeded in keeping the oncoming riders behind him and at a distance.

Again he triggered the old Colt forty-four, missing despite the fact the riders had drawn nearer. He was simply no expert with a pistol and he knew it, and that lack combined with the motion of the rushing stage and the distance that separated him from his targets, was producing poor results. But the outlaws were respecting his efforts nevertheless, and seemed none too anxious to draw closer —at least for the moment.

Remington fired once more, pressed the trigger a second time, and heard the click of the hammer, either on an empty cylinder or a dead cartridge. It could be the latter, he realized; he hadn't used the weapon in a long time and the ammunition was old.

Turning back around, crouched low to make as poor a target of himself as possible, he put his attention on the team. He had felt the horses begin to slow, knew they had given him their best in that first mile or so and that there was no more left in them. He could call on them again and they would do their utmost to respond but their ability would fall short of their willingness. Their reserve was gone.

He raised his eyes to the smoke haze hanging in the distance. Springerville could not be far now, probably around the bend that lay ahead. If he could hold off the outlaws for another few minutes he'd have them beaten—but to do that he'd need to reload his pistol.

That would take a bit of doing. He dare not slack off on the lines still held in his left hand. At the slightest relaxation the team would instantly pull down; and thumbing cartridges from his belt, removing the spent casings from the cylinder of the weapon and replacing them would have to be done with only his free hand. Meanwhile the outlaws, no longer faced with gunfire on his part would guess what was taking place and increase their efforts to draw abreast the stage.

Shaking his head to dislodge the sweat clouding his eyes, Remington braced himself. He'd have to try. Continuing to manage the flagging team with his left hand, he drew his knees together and opening the loading gate of the pistol with a thumb, he pointed it upright, revolved the cylinder with the same thumb and let the fired cartridges fall clear.

When it was empty, he wedged it between his knees, cast a hurried glance at the outlaws now steadily moving up, and pressing fresh cartridges from the loops of his belt, fed them into the pistol. He didn't take time to supply all six openings in the cylinder; he'd best throw a couple of quick shots at the riders, let them know he was still able to hold them off.

Snapping the gate shut, Remington shouted encouragement to the fading team, turned, and snapped two bullets at the outlaws. The second was lucky. He saw one of the men wince, swing off the road and slow. Evidently he wasn't badly hurt, only winged, but he was out of it.

Remington grinned tautly. The remaining outlaws were slacking off—giving up. He'd beaten them again, and he was bringing in his passengers and his team as he was charged to do.

He put his attention back on the road, felt a surge of surprise as he saw the town immediately ahead and realized the horses had swept around the bend he'd seen and were turning into the end of Springerville's main street.

He'd never entered the settlement from the east before, but always on the Apache Springs road which led more or less to the northwest. He saw people along the wide street pause, staring in wonder at the worn, foam-caked horses and the battered, dusty, bullet-pocked coach, boot cover flapping, sweat-stained driver hunched on the perch, eyes switching back and forth as he searched for the stage depot.

They came to an intersection. Remington's probing gaze caught sight of the livery stable, and then the hotel where he ordinarily spent the night off a short ways to his right, and veered the team toward them. The depot would be on the next corner.

22

As he drew to a halt in front of the Valley Lines office and depot Remington saw Jeremiah Crenshaw, the company's owner, standing just inside the open doorway. Next to him was Abe Washington, the station agent. Both men were staring at him in surprise and disbelief.

Two hostlers came running up, equally taken back by the over-all wretched appearance of the coach and its horses as well as the fact he'd arrived on the wrong road. Both were yelling questions.

"Got some passengers that're bad hurt!" he replied, ignoring their inquiries. "Go fetch the doc—and the sheriff!"

Crenshaw and Washington were out on the landing fronting the building and several bystanders had closed in. Crenshaw, his snowy beard thrust straight out like a horizontal icicle, concern in his eyes, nodded briskly to Sam, and stepping up to the door of the stagecoach, yanked it open and looked inside.

"Some of you men," he snapped, pulling back out of the way and making a sweeping gesture with his arm, "lend a hand here, carry these two fellows over to Doc's office. Best we don't wait till he gets here. Hurry it up now!"

Remington, on the ground, and with the babbling hostlers at his heels, was moving slowly along the worn horses, standing with legs apart and heads down. Only Curly, the near wheel horse and never one to show the effects of a hard day's work, seemed to notice the excitement teeming about them and the coach.

"I want them looked after right—and I sure mean right," Sam said, running a hand along Prince's neck. The slim chestnut was trembling and his muzzle and eyes were caked with yellow dust. "I want them watered—they ain't had any since leaving Apache Springs. Then you rub them down and grain them. They've had one hell of a long day."

"Sure, Sam, they'll get it, but why'd you—"

"I'll be coming by the stable soon's I get my feet back under me to look them over."

"All right, Sam, but ain't them bullet holes in the coach?"

"They are," Remington said. He turned to face Abe Washington who had stepped up beside him.

"Coming in from the east," the agent said, a deep frown on his heavy features, "I just can't understand that unless you come over Skull Pass."

"What I done—had to—"

"You wanting me?"

Sam came about. It was the lawman he'd summoned. "Outlaws, up the road a piece—this side of the mountains. Maybe you can lay them by the heels if you get out there quick," he said, and gave the man a hurried summary of what had occurred.

When the sheriff had moved off, shouting for volunteers to make up a posse, Washington again caught at his arm.

"I was asking you about Skull Pass—"

"That was the only way I could get away from that

bunch—and they was dead set on lynching the judge, one of the passengers. It was either take the old road or we was all dead. They kept dogging my dust, even had to finally turn off and come down the side of the mountain to the flat. It was mostly for nothing, howsomever. They was there waiting for us."

Washington was listening, open-mouthed. The hostlers had unhooked the traces from the singletrees, released the tongue, and were leading the exhausted horses off to the stable behind the depot. And Remington, now feeling the full, solid weight of weariness, and in no mind to go into further details relative to the day's events at that moment, pivoted tiredly and returned to the landing. The baggage, removed from the boot of the coach, was now lined up along its edge awaiting claimants.

Two dozen or more persons were still milling about, looking over the stagecoach, talking among themselves, while down the street several others had gathered in front of the doctor's office.

"I aim to go to the hotel, check myself in, and stretch out on the bed for a spell," Remington said. "Then I figure to get myself the biggest steak supper there is around. . . . One thing, soon as you get word from the doc on how them two passengers made out, I'll sure be obliged if you'll let me know."

"Be glad to, Sam," Washington said, clawing at the stubble on his chin. "I just don't savvy none of this. Jeremiah said you'd quit, that there'd be a new driver bringing in the stage—"

"Yeh, young fellow by the name of Billy McElroy. Outlaws killed him when they first jumped us—back up the other side of Halverson's."

"And you took over—"

"Wasn't nothing else to do."

"Well, you sure are leaving in a blaze of glory! Too bad you're doing that. Ain't going to be the same with some other jasper setting up there on the box."

"Man gets too old for the job—leastwise that's what the boss says."

"That was Gavin Crenshaw said that, not Jeremiah."

"It all adds up to the same."

Remington picked up his suitcase and started to move off. Several men in the crowd called out to him, expressing their congratulations, asking questions. He jerked a thumb at Washington.

"Done made my report to Abe. He can tell you what you're wanting to know."

"Maybe not all of it," Jeremiah Crenshaw said, pushing through the gathering and stepping up onto the landing. Lips set, he reached for Sam Remington's hand and shook it vigorously.

"Those women there in Doc's office, Mrs. Longwell and the young one, Mrs. Blackburn, they told me all about what happened. They wanted me to thank you in case they didn't get the chance. Said none of them'd be alive if it hadn't been for you."

"How's the judge and the boy doing?" Remington asked, frowning.

"Doc says they'll make it. Boy's got a concussion and the judge lost a lot of blood, but he figures they'll be all right." Crenshaw paused, eyed Sam critically. "There anything wrong with you? You hurt anywhere?"

"Nope, nothing more'n being a mite tired."

"I reckon you ought to be. It takes a man made out of iron to do what you did—drive that six-up through Skull Pass, then take it straight down the side of the mountain when you saw them outlaws coming at you again. The judge's wife said there was times when the coach was near standing on end but you still kept it going and never once let it turn over."

"Had a good team—"

"Sure you did but it takes horse savvy to get the best out of them without killing them—along with plenty of know-how to keep a coach on its wheels. . . . Now, what're your plans?"

"Aim to do a little resting up then catch the stage for Santa Fe—"

Jeremiah Crenshaw shook his head. "You ain't quitting me, Sam. I won't let you."

"It wasn't my idea—your boy, Gavin—"

"I'll take care of Gavin. I want to hear you say right here and now that you'll forget about quitting and keep on driving for me."

Remington shrugged uncertainly. "I ain't so sure it'd be a good idea. I'm sort've getting along in years—"

"Bosh!" Crenshaw snapped, and then added, "I almost forgot. Those two women said to tell you that soon as their men folks are able, they're going back. Ain't sure what it means but I reckon you do."

Sam Remington smiled. The judge had decided to return, stand up to his responsibilities. Stacey Blackburn was making the same decision, planning to stick by Travis, help him realize his ambition to become a rancher. They weren't quitting—and he'd been the one to point out that to do so was wrong. He reckoned he'd best listen to his own words.

"You savvy what they're talking about?" Crenshaw asked.

The old driver nodded. "Just a little jawing we done together."

"I see. You staying on the job? I need you, Sam."

"Guess I'll be staying, then," Remington replied. "A man's wrong to quit when he's needed."